S0-BCY-464

TRANSFER

A NOVEL BY JERRY FURLAND

Copyright © Gerald K. Furland
All rights reserved.

ISBN: 0-9675322-0-5

Published by
INTECH MEDIA
USA
1999

For volume discounts contact:
INTECH MEDIA
Phone: 423-842-4112
FAX: 423-843-9375
www.intechmedia.net
e-mail: intech@voy.net

Comments and individual copies available:
www.Foilhat.com

Contents

Author's Note

This is a work of fiction. As such, the intent is to entertain. In order to tell the story, familiar organizations or personalities will appear. Having said that, rest assured that none of the fictional characters are real. Any similarity between the fictional characters in this novel, and actual persons living or dead, is coincidental.

This book is dedicated to
Norman L. Blemaster
It was time. . . .

ACKNOWLEDGMENT

To my friends who offered encouragement, and most especially to my family, for putting up with me, thank you.

INTRODUCTION

"This is not the end. It is not even the beginning of the end. But it may be the end of the beginning."

"TRANSFER" is a look forward to one possible future, or as the Director of the ubiquitous Infrastructure Protection Task Force would prefer to say, "end-state scenario."

In this, the first of three volumes, a new economy borne of cutting edge technological progress is about to change forever the relationship between America and its citizens.

It has often been argued that technology is essentially neutral. The possibilities, agendas if you will, that technology can be harnessed to serve, arguably are not.

Fortunately, TRANSFER is, after all, just fiction.

CHAPTER ONE

HIDTA HQ Boston, MA.
December 14, 2008

Finding time for himself wasn't getting any easier. John O'dea, Intelligence Branch Chief for the Boston High Intensity Drug Trafficking Area (HIDTA), looked one more time at the first quarter, fiscal year 2008, intelligence threat summary, grimacing over an olive tinged cup of tepid fluid that several hours earlier might have passed for coffee. He was almost through. It was less than two weeks to Christmas. The presents he had yet to buy for his children would have to be mailed. Now that his son and daughter were grown and had moved on to lives of their own, home for John O'dea was a comfortable flat above a model sailing ship museum on Atlantic Avenue, two blocks from his office in downtown Boston.

The marriage had ended in divorce, mutually desired, before Chris and Melanie were in high school. All in all, he had done okay raising them alone. He had done right by Victoria too. Despite the divorce they were civil in their dealings with each other. The generosity of the cash settlement he offered Victoria let him keep the house and raise the kids. Their home, sun and salt weathered, anchored in the sandy soil of the cape, was just a summer rental property now, managed for him by a resort properties broker in Plymouth.

After the divorce, Victoria had retreated into the Boston Yankee Brahmin society of her old moneyed family and eventually remarried. John had not. They seldom spoke and, like the commuters' nightmare that was Boston during the Christmas season, his failed marriage was no longer a burden to him.

Glancing out the window to the traffic jam seven stories below, he knew he would be home in five minutes - four if he walked briskly. There used to be a gym on the fourth floor of his building. When the last of the U.S. Coast Guard District staff moved out, they took the equipment with them. '*Budget cuts. Deeper every year.*'

He could leave anytime. He had more than his twenty years in. It was the work he did that mattered, more so than the pay. For John O'dea the work was everything. It was a chess game, a puzzle of endless variation. And, it was ending. John rubbed his eyes and leaned back in his chair. '*Happy New Year, and may you live in interesting times my friend. At least the Cape House was paid off.*'

The joy of his work was the gamesmanship. Mano y mano. The game was ending. The game wouldn't have been fun if the opposing team, the international drug trafficking cartels, money launderers, and their corrupt, well paid attorneys had been stupid. Now, stupid or smart, nothing could save them.

And to think that New Years Eve, 1999 had been such a big deal. Compared to the imminent New Years Eve in the year of our Lord, 2009, New Years Eve 1999 barely rated a yawn. Despite certain academics who had smugly asserted that the new millennium was still "mathematically" a year away, the popular view was and remained, that it began at midnight of New Years Eve, 1999.

The report was done. It was already past seven in the evening. John was tired. The Office of National Drug Control Policy (ONDCP) in Washington would review and archive this likely, last of a kind, quarterly intelligence report from Boston HIDTA headquarters. A keystroke would send it on its way. John snapped off the terminal and stepped into the hallway. To him it seemed the hoopla of 1999 had only masked the real "Big Deal" of the new millennium.

The big deal really began January 2, 2001. With remarkably little fanfare, the seed was planted that would bloom across the entire nation eight years later. State government employees performed the work, toiling thanklessly in motor vehicle registration offices throughout the country. What they were doing, banal, repetitive, drudge work, was the seminal beginning of the real dawn of the new millennium, implemented in the relentless pursuit of order.

The funny thing was, Bostonians, telecast "live" in the local "Eye Witness News" segment, bitched mostly about the incredibly snail paced movement of what everyone agreed was the longest line they had stood in since the 1996 Patriots Super Bowl season. The mandatory fingerprinting and revised six-page application were largely accepted with typical Bostonian cynicism as just one more example of pencil pushing, bullshit stupidity. The new biometrics technology combination drivers license/national ID, and "smart" card had already been sold to the public as absolutely necessary. John had resented it more than most. The fact that his "significant other," Dawn Fenstermacher, had played a "significant role" in the creation of the new card had helped him keep his thoughts to himself. In any event, Dawn worked as many hours as John did. By mutual agreement they rarely discussed details of their work with each other.

It had begun to snow. Along the waterfront, snow streaked sideways, nearly horizontal in the bitter wind off the bay. Leaving the building, John hunched his shoulders involuntarily as the cold searched for an opening. '*Maybe they would order in tonight.*' He could build a nice log fire in the fireplace and uncork a dry Spanish Red.

Dawn was a big woman, with a decidedly not anorexic figure. Of solid Bavarian stock (her family left Germany in the depression years following the First World War), she had been blessed with a perfect complexion and a lustrous mane of dark brown hair, which she still wore shoulder length. She typically wore reading glasses, half lens, wire framed, which gave her a somewhat professorial appearance, entirely at odds with what was at forty-four years of age, still a damn fine looking body. Five feet, ten inches in stockings, when she kissed John, (who was just a shade over six feet), standing up, they were nearly eye to eye.

Several years ago marriage had been discussed and discreetly shelved. She had said, "John, I love you dearly and you are the sweetest man I have ever known, but I'll be damned if I am going to be saddled with a name like "Dawn O'dea." I'm sorry darling, I truly am, but Dawn O'dea is a bit much, isn't it? Let's enjoy what we have. We're not kids anymore. You don't have to worry about making me an honest woman."

'*She was right*' he thought as he grabbed the mail from the box on the landing. More catalogs - so much for the demise of snail mail - '*Tuscany Woods,*' *Free Delivery, $5.00 Off Any Large Pizza. Done!*' Entering the flat he grabbed the cell phone and a box of long matches, dialing the number even as he stooped to light the fire.

***

Nascent Resources Group Corporation
Boston Field Division
Federal Reserve Building, Boston, MA

Dawn Fenstermacher had been a pioneering software developer in the early eighties for a certain company that grew to control over 80 percent of the global market.

She had managed to emerge intact from the Silicon Valley insanity of the late nineties, a millionaire many times over. Married, divorced, remarried and widowed, Dawn had been through some changes.

Her first husband, Darren Faehnrich, was dreaming his life away in a long-term care, substance abuse rehab facility in San Jose. A combination of cocaine addiction and a nervous breakdown had destroyed her young husband, a man whose ground breaking achievements in electron beam litho-engraving technology generated royalties, expectations and a "take it to the limit" lifestyle far beyond his midwestern farm boy's capacity to sustain.

Exhausted emotionally and mentally, he had collapsed soon after his process was applied to produce the first generation of 1.7 GHZ, 512M SDRAM "monster" chips - a four fold increase over the fastest and highest capacity Random Access Memory devices in existence at the time.

One day, about seven years ago, he had refused to leave the house and no matter how hard Dawn had tried to reach him, he had gone on a permanent vacation to a place only he could enter and would probably never return from. Royalties and stock in the company were more than sufficient to make his life comfortable. Not that he would likely ever take notice or care.

Her second marriage had lasted less than a year. Her second husband, J. Thomas Webster, "Tommy" to his friends, a free lance venture capitalist, by contrast was a rock of stability. The risk/reward ratio in his line of work negated the need for artificial stimulation. He had died in an automobile accident on Hwy. One. A rainy day and a stalled school bus on a blind corner. Had he not swerved to avoid the bus he would have made it. Air bags can't defeat a 700 foot, free fall into the Pacific Ocean.

So John had once asked her about marriage? She had ample cause to demur. She knew with certainty John loved her, but she also wondered if maybe she had acquired a bit of John O'dea's Gaelic superstition to "leave well enough alone." Like her second husband, her life had been "exciting" enough.

Tonight she had run the sequence again. The ZIZPRO, (Ziggurat, Inverted Ziggurat Protocol,) program software was functioning flawlessly. *Again.* Her attention to detail approached compulsive/obsessive disorder in severity. It had also made her a millionaire by the time she was twenty-eight years old. The problem ZIZPRO was to eliminate was not new. Despite a high degree of standardization in protocols both in the software industry and the Internet, what ZIZPRO required was an order of flexibility approaching omniscience.

ZIZPRO was designed to communicate with, transfer, and manipulate data from virtually every database in the United States, as well as, international databases.

It would operate in real time and seamlessly integrate all requests for financial, medical, legal, business, government, licensing, communications, personal histories, credit, federal, state and municipal entitlements–the entire gamut of every transaction of day to day living in modern society. The world was going paperless and ZIZPRO was the platform to make it all work.

With ZIZPRO there was no need for a monolithic gargantuan central database. Just connect the dots between existing structures and you have it, centralized intelligence in a decentralized network. Once you were in, you could just leave your wallet and purse at home. As long as you had your biometrics smart card or, if you were really with the program, the implant and ultraviolet tattoo, you were set. Never again to fill out an insurance application, credit application, or admissions slip for a visit to the doctor or hospital. Passport, Drivers License, ID Card, Medical and Employment History, Marital Status, Dependents, Deeds, Stocks, Investments and Debts, in essence, everything about you was available in real time, and with the optional, but eventually mandatory implant/ tattoo, you were provided with absolute security from fraud, theft, and forgery.

It still amused her. Five years ago she had conceived the basic structure of the software/operating system and hardware as a result of a casual lunch time conversation in the company commissary with a young woman named Tammy Davidson. A single mother, struggling to get by on secretary pay, Tammy had asked Dawn if she would explain how a computer really works.

"I know it sounds kinda stupid, but I want to help April, she's my little girl, to understand all this stuff and I don't even know how to explain it to myself."

She had explained that although her daughter was just three years old, Tammy hoped she might grow up to be like Dawn and the "others" some day, leaving "not just a secretary like me" unsaid.

Dawn had thought, '*yes, it does sound 'kinda stupid.*'

But, with no children of her own, Dawn had been touched by this young mother's desire to teach her child and her high hopes for her little girl's future.

She thought for a moment and said, "it's really not all that hard Tammy. Have April try to imagine a water tower. The water tower has water in it for everyone to use and pipes to take the water into the homes of all the people who are connected. They open the faucet and the water comes out. Computers do the same thing with information. It stores information and anyone with the right connection and a faucet can use it."

That night, Dawn had lain awake at the edge of sleep, musing idly about a little girl's imagination, wondering if maybe she had been just a little too simple in her attempt to draw a preschool level analogy. That's when it had come to her. An image of a water tower, a special one, with discrete levels you could access by means of interconnected piping attached to the sides of the cylinder that rose in a circular fashion–sort of like a temple building she remembered from where-- '*Sunday school, and what was it they had called that temple. . . it was called a . . . ziggurat! Yes! That was it, a ziggurat, unlike a pyramid, it rose cylindrically in a continuous ramp. Why, anyone could see that if the levels were stacked, then connections between the levels could be made by selecting one or two or any combination of levels. . . .'*

She had sat up in bed. *'There was a structure here. Like a nautilus shell in one respect, but that wasn't it really. . . the structure would have to be. . . yes, and if sandwiched and inverted, stacked in mirror image, with the pipes vertically feeding and drawing water or data it would facilitate. . . .'*

By then she had groped for the light and grabbed a notebook from the night stand. Rough sketching a diagram, *'the code could select here or here, or everywhere, or just one, as applicable to the task - sure, it made perfect sense! You could even use the structure to efficiently share tasking from a variety of protocols, even network these for massively processing data and eliminating,'* "SEQUENCE COMPLETE, ALL APPLICATIONS FUNCTIONING" startled her from her reverie. It was getting late. *'John would be worried.'* She placed a "be home in fifteen" message to John on her digital assistant and called for her driver, one of the perks. John had kind of wrinkled his nose at the thought, but he had to admit he didn't mind her being seen safely home each evening.

She took the escalator down to the Lobby. Seeing the gathering blizzard, her last thought as she passed her hand through the scanner to exit the security barrier was *'we should order in tonight.'* The driver opened her door as the snow swirled in the luminescent glare of the city.

***

Boston College

David Chandler wasn't going home for Christmas this year, a first. The strangeness of it adding to the homesickness he had experienced off and on since coming to Boston a year ago. Whip thin and hard muscled; David was, pound for pound, one of the best rowers in the country. That and a couple of dollars might get you a very small cup of coffee he thought as he locked the boathouse and fumbled stiff fingered with the security alarm keypad. "I must be out of my mind!" he said to no one in particular. This was not just cold; this was bone aching, nut shriveling, freezer burn torture.

Back home in Soddy Daisy, Tennessee, his sisters and parents would be tooling around in light jackets or even just a sweater and a scarf doing some last minute shopping and braving the mid fifties, even low sixties temperatures - '*shit, they were probably still mowing the grass!*,' but David had a dream. Too light to man an oar, he drove himself just the same. As coxswain, he had captained the Boston College team to the regional championship.

Now working with some of the best amateur rowers in the country, they, yes they–all twelve rowers and the six alternates and himself, were going to make the U.S. Nationals, or he thought smiling grimly, die of hypothermia trying. David was not just a dumb jock, and crew was not football. Speed, discipline, agility, endurance and brains-he had it all. What he didn't have, and probably never would, despite his commitment, was the raw power required to pull an oar in Olympic level competition. David would always be thin and at just five feet, nine inches he tipped the scales at barely one hundred forty lbs.. A fierce and fearless competitor, he had more than compensated by becoming the most respected coxswain and admired young coach on the eastern seaboard.

Before coming to Boston he never really swore much. David never swore in front of his family. He felt the same nagging guilt about swearing that he did when occasionally - rarely, "almost never," he reminded himself, had a beer or two watching the games on sundays with some of his more worldly teammates.

David's Dad, Art Chandler, was a successful small businessman and lay Methodist preacher, now retired, who had realized his dream of owning a piece of land with good water and timber and enough pasturage and cleared acreage to become a "gentleman farmer." Tucked away in the foothills of Soddy Daisy below Signal Mountain, his one hundred thirty acre spread was just a short drive north and west of the "scenic" city of Chattanooga, Tennessee.

Art Chandler was a decorated Viet Nam War veteran–a LRRP–Long Range Reconnaissance Patrol-squad leader who had both seen and inflicted death. Art was a good man. John O'dea, who had been his radio operator and best friend, had known that first hand. On a "heavy stick" vertical insertion, all the way into Cambodia, John had collapsed from a combination of heat exhaustion and dysentery. In the middle of an ambush of a battalion of NVA regulars that had gone seriously awry, Art, wounded by mortar shrapnel, had half-dragged, half-carried John under heavy enemy fire to the extraction zone and saved his life. Of the twelve man "stick," four made it home.

Now that David was away from home and on his own in Boston, Art had asked John to "look in" on David from time to time. John was only too happy to serve, inviting David to spend Christmas with him and Dawn.

'John's okay,' David thought as he half ran to his battered white '98 Civic Hatchback. David appreciated that he had a place to go on Christmas Day, and Dawn was a helluva nice lady too. He would have to pick up a few things.

The car lugged a little before starting and then roared to life, its perforated muffler giving the lie to what was just a little four banger in reality. He had night class across town, dual MBA program-- Computer Science and Business. David's thesis was a paper on the impact of microchip photonics and the maturation of asynchrous transfer mode–ATM–technology on global communications and international commerce in the 21st century. Darting into a split second opportunity to join the stream of late rush hour traffic, David hoped the heat would kick in soon. Like his father's old army buddy, John O'dea, time, for David, was a precious commodity.

**

December 16, 2008
Soddy Daisy, Tennessee

The new joists were solid and Art was pleased. Come early summer, the first mowing would half fill the refurbished hay mow above the mountain stone and timber barn. Art Chandler, fifty-eight years old, still moved with the springy assurance of a man twenty-five years younger. When he was David's age, he could run a mile with a forty lb. pack in just over four minutes. Undoing the accumulation of years of neglect on a property this large, with a six-bedroom house, barn, machine shed, stable and well house, had taken a little longer.

Art was a self-educated man; his children were the first Chandlers to even attend college. "Measure twice, cut once," was as applicable to his dealings with others as to his careful and exacting carpentry. People trusted Art and when he spoke, in his careful measured way, they listened.

Sturdy in mind and spirit, he had set to himself a standard of obedience and reverence to God and service to His Word. He had not always been so. There had been a time in his life when the Word had been distant. Still, God's plan for him would not be denied.

There was the violence and moral chaos of Viet Nam. There had been women, too many women. Art had a "way" about him, something hard to describe or even define, but there it was, and women had responded. Of course, there were the drinking and tobacco too. God waited.

Home from Viet Nam, the transition to civilian life had proceeded rather effortlessly. He had been good at his job. Actually, he had been more than good. The Army had tried every blandishment to keep him. They had offered free college, a commission, and his choice of duty stations, to no avail. Art, even then, was a man not plagued by self-doubt. He had no doubts about leaving the army. Then he met Betty.

Their first meeting was not memorable. Introduced to Art at a fourth of July barbecue by a mutual acquaintance, Betty had been put off by what she considered to be an excess of self-confidence. In turn, Art had dismissed her as too prim and proper by half a grade school teacher! Art's school memories were not fond ones. He had managed to graduate from high school with a bare minimum of effort and an overwhelming sense of gratitude when it was over. Home from the war in Indochina and free to do as he chose, Art was not particularly interested in anything like a serious relationship or emotional commitment. They would not see each other again for an entire year when, at the home of another mutual acquaintance, they had found themselves engaged in a not entirely unpleasant conversation. He had called her the following week and to both their surprises, she had accepted his invitation to dinner. More dates followed in the weeks to come.

Betty had seen something in Art–something good and true, a special Inner Light, that she was certain, could be nurtured and helped to shine and grow. In the end, it was Betty who had proposed and Art, bemused at this turn of events, perhaps even then sensing that God had waited long enough, accepted. They married the following month.

They had purchased the farm property twelve years ago. Collecting the scrap ends of lumber destined for kindling, Art let his mind wander back to a July afternoon in 1996, the passage of time a blur of images and colors, his children grown and his children as children. Their daughters, Tracy and Suzy, had been away on a youth group trip to Washington, D.C., and David was attending summer Bible camp. The house empty, he and Betty had packed a picnic basket and headed out of the city–no particular destination in mind.

They had turned west off route 153 to follow the arrow on the hand painted "For Sale by Owner" sign. The "road" had been rough graded and graveled by the county, but not oiled, and the dust rising in the summer heat billowed in a cloud behind their pickup truck, the loose pea gravel clattering in the wheel wells. Twisting and doubling back on itself, the road climbed a ridge through old growth timber, crossed a small wooden trestle bridge, and seemingly having spent itself in the effort, abruptly ended half a mile beyond.

A pellet riddled mailbox stood sentry at the intersection of a dirt driveway marked with another hand lettered sign proclaiming "Private Drive--No Trespassing," with the ubiquitous, "For Sale by Owner," recently painted across the bottom of the board. The ratchet buzz of cicadas and staccato jackhammer of a hungry woodpecker floated in the hazy air, heavy, and green scented with the lushness of the late summer afternoon. Betty, a woman of rare intellect, had looked at her husband's face, and had known in that moment, that this was going to be to be their home.

Art finished at the woodpile. With a last look at the gables of the old barn in the deepening dusk, he turned toward the house. This late in the year night came early and cold. "Maybe David will call tonight," he said to no one in particular. A lonely first star in the thin blue winter sky seemed to wink in agreement as Art trudged along. The door opened bright and warm, smells of baking and good things simmering on the stove. Art shut the door and bent to unlace his work boots. 'Those timbers are going to be just fine.'

***

CHAPTER TWO

December 17, 2008
Shelter Island, New York

Ben Gladding had bought a seat on the COMEX in the early eighties. He had been a cover boy on several of the nation's most respected business magazines. Ben's talent was arbitrage. Ben was a currency "bookie."

Ben traded in currencies, buying a foreign currency or capital instrument when it suited his needs and selling when the sale could generate a profit. "Short" or "long" whenever he traded, he usually won. He was a Wall Street legend before he turned thirty.

In the final run to 1999 and the advent of the "Euro" in the Western European Union (WEU) he had, with few exceptions, been on the "right" side of every exchange, netting huge profits as a result. In the three years following the introduction of the Euro, Ben had played the chaos of political and fiscal maneuvering amongst the WEU nations and the ebb and tide of intra-European exchange rates with unprecedented skill and luck. Speed was paramount. Recognition of windows of opportunity that could open and close in the time it takes to smoke a cigarette, was his special gift.

Ben was often described as a prick, but no one did it better. The Securities and Exchange Commission (SEC) had always taken a lively interest in what Ben Gladding was doing, had done and was about to do. In fact, what Ben was about to do on any given day, in large part, tended to drive the rates of exchange in the short term, despite the fact that longer term trends were driven by less malleable realities of international macroeconomics. Ben had emigrated from the city to the more comfortable environs of Shelter Island, NY. His commute to the city to ply his trade long since negated by the capability to be anywhere on the globe digitally and in real time. Ben loved the new cyber-currency.

The "Euro" had largely died stillborn as a new issue of legal tender within the European Common Market. It was stupid, not the notion of a single currency, the notion that the Euro would be a printed paper currency--a last gasp of printing press era technologies and economics in a new age of digital transactions. For many, the Euro existing in tandem with national currencies--with dual prices for goods and services listed in, for example, Francs and Euros--had been confusing and burdensome.

Ben had ridden the financial swells in both directions with equal enthusiasm. The "bloodletting" in the capital markets of Europe had been a thing of great joy and wondrous beauty. He had, with extraordinary consistency, anticipated and profited by every death rattle of the Common Market's national currencies as the paper Euro and most recently, the digital Euro led to their ultimate extinction. Europe had gone digital in 2008. The Asian markets were edging to a goal of 2015. The United States would go digital January 1, 2009. As each transformation occurred there was opportunity for profit in the ensuing chaos.

"How much is enough," when it came to making money was a question Ben would consider absurd–no, asinine. Ben never tired of making more and as far as he was concerned, never would. The markets were fluctuating wildly. Ben calibrated success in hundredths of percentage points. Exchange fluctuations of late had more than satisfied his minimums for advances and declines. He bought and sold in millions of dollars on each trade–laying off a "loser" to those less nimble and taking a new position that invariably accentuated the bleak future of the last transaction, as well as, magnifying the very bright future of his newly acquired position.

Ben still had some immediate groundwork ahead of him, even though his staff was already well prepared for 2009. Lucrative arrangements with key foreign banking institutions and currency markets were largely "in the can." The "personal touch" of a Ben Gladding visit would still be needed to seal these very private arrangements and to ensure the enthusiastic cooperation of certain highly placed foreign officials who were central to the overall game plan. A huge sense of satisfaction buoyed his spirits on this blustery winter day. Ben's time was coming and the sheer scale of his future earnings would dwarf even his greatest achievements. *'Life was sweet.'*

***

December 18, 2007
Washington, D.C.
IPTF Command Center

The triumph of the 2000 elections had cemented the Republican Party's control of the national political leadership. The current administration was basking in the warmth of two successive terms in the White House in which the state of the economy, public education, and opportunity for all Americans had clearly eclipsed even the most wildly optimistic expectations of both conventional and unconventional wisdom in the national media.

WOW

The heir apparent for the Presidency of the United States, Vice President James Dustin Waites (J.D. Waites), had achieved a landslide victory in the November elections in a lopsided contest against a confused and ineffectual opponent.

The Democratic Party, plagued with legal as well as financial woes, had been saddled with a candidate who consistently failed to frame even a single issue of sufficient resonance or broad appeal among the majority of the voters.

The old coalition of minorities, unions, federal and state employees and the elderly, comprising the traditional base of the Party, had splintered. The robust American economy and sweeping global changes of the early 21st century had accrued to the general benefit of the American voters and they voted their pocketbooks for the Republican Party.

In the weeks ahead the transition teams would be focused on the transfer of power to the incoming administration. The swearing in ceremony of President-elect J.D. Waites and Vice President-elect Marion Young promised to be a national celebration of epic proportion as America looked to a bright and prosperous future. The new President was determined to keep it that way. His Cabinet appointments, a large number of which were reshuffles from the previous administration, reflected his caution to not upset the apple cart with too many new faces.

Tim Thurston, Captain, USN(retired), reviewed his notes from his late night session alone with the new Chief Executive. The meeting had gone well. Tim had submitted a pro-forma letter of resignation as Director of the Infrastructure Protection Task Force (IPTF). Of course, J.D. Waites had refused to accept Tim's resignation. He had also refused the resignation of Tim's Deputy, James Dodd. It was largely Jim Dodd's information technology industry contacts and the considerable savvy of those contacts that had ensured the technical execution of IPTF goals and objectives.

As a result, Tim Thurston had been free to concentrate on the equally daunting and extraordinarily sensitive, political, legal and ethical challenges the IPTF agenda would create.

Yesterday, Tim had briefed the president-elect in his office in the old Executive Building staying on to talk late into the night without interruption. When alone, they were simply "Tim" and "J.D.," each comfortable with the other and in near total agreement on the relevant issues of the day.

The interview had begun with the president-elect rising from behind his desk and ushering Tim to a pair of overstuffed wing chairs flanking a low coffee table set for tea. "So tell me Tim, how the hell are you? Can I get you some tea or would you like something a little stronger?"

The combination of J.D.'s smile and "let's just visit over a backyard barbecue" manner was completely disarming to the uninitiated. Even for Tim, the incredible pull of the man and the desire to please and ingratiate oneself had not, despite long association, been dulled. J.D. Waites was the hands-down acknowledged master of charm, whether one on one or speaking to an auditorium. You just couldn't help it. Everyone who had ever met the president-elect invariably came away persuaded that he or she really had experienced a special and personal connection with the man.

"Thanks J.D., I'll have a Scotch if you're having one. By the way, I have to agree with the 'talking heads" on TV last night. At the press conference yesterday you hit the goddamn ball right out of the park."

He handed Tim a heavy leaded crystal tumbler, and motioned for him to take a seat, "You really think so? Sometimes I wonder Tim. There are still more than a few critics out there who believe this transition is some sinister conspiracy to enslave the American people."

The President sat down across from Tim and leaned forward intently, "Where are your folks going with this deal Tim? We can't afford to be complacent. Hell, you and I both know how quick opinions can turn. That lip chewing, lying sack of shit thought he was free and clear right up…."

Trailing off in mid sentence was a habit of the president-elect when dealing with unpleasant outcomes. With a sigh the President-elect settled back into the wing chair, and rubbed his eyes. When he opened them again, he had looked hard at Tim and said, "Let us both be absolutely clear on this. When the shit hits the fan Tim, it better not spray the White House or me."

Tim had answered soothingly, "I understand completely. Let me give you the quick and dirty now, and we can delve deeper at any point you wish. As you know, the transition team has been brought up to speed on IPTF operations, methods, objectives etc."

"We are keeping a low profile on most of the data taken from the 'stream.' The Prime Contractor, Nascent Resources Group, assures me that all twelve regions in the Federal Reserve System are wired in and operational. Security on the clipper protocol and the ZIZPRO Protocol host program has been leak proof. I do not, repeat, do not, anticipate any concerns about security. All Cabinet Departments understand the special role of the IPTF and we have not encountered any serious difficulties. Justice and Defense, as you recall, gave us some grief during the first term of your predecessor but those issues are long resolved."

Tim reached into his briefcase and pulled out a thick binder of folders, all marked with code word digraphs and the caveat "DIRECTOR/IPTF/EYES ONLY."

"Again, to cut to the chase, our main areas of concern here are public opinion and proper education of that opinion. My staff has been working with all the Cabinet Secretaries, the Hill leadership and their staffs. We've negated most of the opposition with the help of certain files we have obtained. Our political allies as well as our opponents both on the Hill and in the media have been clearly identified. The Print Media and the Net are potential trouble spots, the Net more so. Hell, nobody reads the newspaper anymore and the papers that do have influence are mostly sympathetic to our program. Targeting options and other strategies for dealing with serious media difficulties are ready to execute as appropriate."

Tim handed the folders to the President, "These OPLANS project response's, appropriate to a variety of outcome, or as we like to call them, "end state" scenarios–six in all. They are flexible, can be combined in whole or in part and are continuously updated in real time to reflect current positions."

Tim leaned back and gestured, palms up, "No system is fail-safe J.D. and I won't guarantee a painless transition for your administration or for all citizens. We will manage the pain, keep it under control and deal with the problems according to plan. When the dust settles, you and the American people will be standing together. On that you have my word."

The President-elect of the United States slipped back into his "next door neighbor" persona "Hell Tim, I know that, and you know you have my fullest support. You also know I expect, no, insist you keep me apprized at all times and that means up close and personal. The Chief of Staff, security detail and my personal secretary have each been briefed on this. They all understand that you are on my immediate access list."

The President-elect walked to the silver drink service cart and busied himself with ice cubes and scotch, "It's gonna be a hell of a ride Tim, but I'm betting on you to take us across the finish line." He sat down again across from Tim and handed him a refurbished scotch on the rocks, "Now, let's have another drink and talk about this one." The President had opened up the top file in the stack marked 'RENAISSANCE.'

"RENAISSANCE" was the jewel in Thurston's crown as Director of the IPTF. The cultural, societal, fiscal and financial impact of the dismantling of America's legal tender based on printed paper currency and minted coin was enormous. In effect, the government was wiping the slate clean. Digital currency placed the ultimate tool for social engineering solely in the government's grasp. Perhaps weapon was more apt a metaphor than tool.

Tim had run down the high points for the president-elect. RENAISSANCE would be the process of rebirth or reclamation of "destructive" elements in society that were to be disenfranchised under the new system. RENAISSANCE itself had been long in existence. It was both spin and operational planning for the new cash-less society and sought to anticipate as well as implement the appropriate programs and policies necessary to deal with the consequences of a cash-less society.

RENAISSANCE had skillfully spun every milestone toward the eventual abolishment of paper currency through its media allies. All federal employees and military personnel had been on direct deposit since the mid-1980's. In fact the military especially had been the platform of choice for beta testing the RENAISSANCE programs. In 1997 an entire military installation had gone digital. The officers and soldiers alike, had been issued "smart" cards for use at all Base retail stores, travel arrangements, medical and dental visits, processing of orders and service record entries. It was hailed as a huge success.

Another beta test for future civilian applications was in the procurement of fingerprint readers. Since 1998 all military personnel, active duty and reserve, were digitally fingerprinted when they were issued a new identity card. The machine was quite simple, smaller than a pencil sharpener, and sat on the desktop next to the digital camera system. In less time than it takes to tell, the applicant was photographed and fingerprinted, the data stored digitally and a new "ID" emerging from the printer ready to issue.

1999 was the advent of mandatory electronic "direct deposit" for all individuals receiving any form of federal government pension, social security payments, subsidies etc. The government would no longer write a check for these purposes, requiring instead electronic transfers via direct deposit only. Over twenty million recipients had been receiving government payments by check and cashing them without ever having a bank account. In 1998, each had received a pleasant letter from the federal government informing them that effective October 1, 1999, the government would be happy to hold the recipients funds in escrow without interest, but in order to receive the funds, the recipient must open an account for direct deposit. This was implemented with barely a whimper. Direct deposit cost the government three cents per transaction compared to approximately seven dollars in total cost to print and mail each recipient a check. The savings: 140 million dollars per month, almost 1.7 Billion dollars a year with no reduction in benefits. Further savings in operations due to elimination of printing equipment maintenance, mass mailing processing, superfluous physical plant costs and redundant employees saved an additional seven billion dollars per year.

The millennium had brought national biometrics ID cards administered by the states and piggy backed onto motor vehicle operator licenses. Hidden in an innocuous piece of federal legislation back in 1996, a rally by citizens opposed to this potential threat to privacy and freedom had failed. A discreet sharing of the contents of certain sensitive files with the subjects of the files, for instance, several of the key members of Congress especially the leadership and committee chairmen had a remarkable calming effect on the rhetoric of the opposition. Bills were introduced to overturn the ID cards but they never made it to the floor. RENAISSANCE had been well prepared to handle the threat.

Again, the savings were enormous. Losses due to illegal aliens, welfare fraud, payroll fraud and various abuses of entitlements, Medicare and Medicaid, were brought sharply downward within the first twelve months of operations. Savings of over one hundred billion dollars in the first two years were hard to criticize. A majority of the hard-working public had been most appreciative.

Attempts to challenge the national ID program in the courts consistently failed to over turn the legislation. The final death knell was sounded in 2002 by a landmark 7-2 Supreme Court decision (McCallister V Georgia). "The responsibility to safeguard the nations fiscal health and national sovereignty supersedes protection of individual privacy provided any private information gleaned as a result thereof shall not be used by the government, or released by the government, in any manner resulting in an abridgement of any individual's expectation of or enjoyment of the right to privacy."

BAD
LAW

As pieces of the system clicked into place one by one, increasingly, the ability to buy or to sell was accomplished through electronic means. By 2003, virtually all financial instruments, deeds, titles, conveyances, stocks, bonds, coupons, leases, purchases, rents–all transactions involving earnings, pensions, annuities, wages, tips, and capital gains became electronic through the use of electronic withdrawals, debit cards, direct deposit and the like. These digital records fed into integrated databases that by the year 2002 were nearly complete. Once the "system" was loaded, maintenance of the database became routine and only death could remove a record from scrutiny and monitoring.

In October of 2004 a unique identifier had been assigned to each individual. It was a combination of their existing social security number with an additional alpha/numeric identifier used to identify each individual's date of birth, gender, and to track entry into the new system.

Like the old social security number, the new number was non-transferable, permanent and by law, assigned at birth (Social Security Numbers for children and newborns had been required by the federal government since 1996, if parents were intending to claim their children as dependents on their tax returns.

The new number was almost fail-safe, but not quite. It was still too much like a credit card or driver's license. They could be lost or stolen, and despite the difficulty, the technology that created the card was vulnerable to high tech forgery. The disabled—quadriplegics, amputees, and other motor skill impaired citizens—were unable to participate in the system. Work continued. Biometrics technologies were available to embed the identifier in a bar code applied as an ultraviolet scanner visible permanent tattoo. The tattoo was applied to the forehead and to the hand. Naturally, the tattoo was not visible in ordinary light.

All businesses, government offices, health care facilities, law enforcement agencies–local, state and federal, customs and immigration points, were wired in. The IRS, under the omnibus IRS Reorganization Act legislation of 2004, (IRSRA 2005), implemented a reformed tax code simplifying both collection and computation of revenues.

By 2005, the system was digitized, paperless, in practical terms, omniscient. It was capable of tracking and processing the daily financial activity of the world's largest economy. With a national annual GDP of 9.3 trillion dollars and tens of billions of domestic financial transactions daily, the new IRS and its processing center were miracles of digital computer automation.

Under the new economy, Federal and State Income Taxes were no longer prepared by taxpayers on an annual basis. Instead, all taxes due were collected as appropriate, comparative data analyzed and rates adjusted quarterly; payroll, sales taxes, property taxes, FICA, unemployment insurance, capital gains etc., were each accounted for, either collected in whole or amortized (i.e., property taxes) electronically.

Passports, SSN cards, driver's licenses, insurance cards, credit cards, voter registrations, jury duty selections, licenses, fees, permits, were digitally generated and entered into the individuals electronic record. Once one was entered into the system, wallets and purses were only used for photos of children and makeup. All other traditional wallet contents like cash, checks, credit cards, licenses and ID's of every sort were no longer needed. Only the individuals electronic history was needed to gain access to funds, licenses, memberships etc.

A new agency was built on the skeleton of the old United States Dept. of Commerce. Relying on the same technology as the IRS, the revamped agency, fused with and renamed the "International Commerce Commission," tracked all international financial transactions. The concept was much simpler than would be imagined. All that was required was access to the data stream generated by the flow of capital, goods and services across international boundaries. Federal control of the transaction was implicit but not required. The "take" was for purposes of taxation, analysis of trends, and to identify transfers of capital involved in criminal activity.

Decisions as to exchange rates for currencies, intervention to stabilize markets or to head off market conditions inimical to the financial well being of the United States and its Allies were made elsewhere but depended on the

ICC for data. The ICC's main focus was to eliminate illicit trafficking in drugs and contraband by denying access to the cybercurrency system to fund the transaction. Eliminating international money laundering and drug trafficking transactions and the profits they generated were expected to be the first victories for the ICC. The IPTF and RENAISSANCE would quietly pull the strings behind the scenes.

Efficiency in processing currency exchange, credit, travel, health care, rentals, leasing, every day financial transactions to include vending machines, tolls and parking fees as well as traffic tickets, and typical governmental fees for licenses and permits etc. had been increasing exponentially even without the introduction of cybercurrency. With the new technologies in place, the capacity to eliminate paper currency altogether became fully operational in the year 2005. The decision to eliminate all forms of paper money and conveyances was now technically feasible. For the IPTF, execution of the plan was now merely a political issue.

Government revenues were expected to experience an immediate windfall due to the collapse of the "underground" economy. All wages, tips, barter schemes, transactions for products and services would be tracked, accounted for, and taxed at the point of origin. The cost of collection was to be virtually eliminated and enforcement was to be by fiat.

To work, to eat, to survive, you had to be able to buy or sell. If you bought or sold, you were taxed. There was no escape.

By the mid-1990's, the welfare system in the U.S., was already experimenting with welfare debit cards vice cash or vouchers, like food stamps etc. Under the cash-less society, welfare would become fraud free as the bar code only allowed for authorized purchases. The items one purchased were bar coded as well. Rent subsidies, cost of living allowances etc. would, for the first time, be effectively and tightly controlled. Welfare costs would plummet. All unproductive aspects of administering the programs would be slashed to the minimum. RENAISSANCE projected that under the cyber currency system, less than five cents of every welfare dollar would be expended in purely administrative overhead. This compared to as much as seventy-two cents of every government welfare dollar spent on administration under the old system.

The new system allowed all overlapping programs to be combined or eliminated. The potential savings were astronomical. The "sales pitch" practically wrote itself. Dissent was easily quashed at both ends of the political spectrum. How could any reasonably compassionate, responsible individual argue with this kind of efficiency? Or, put another way, morally, how could America not implement a program that protects and even expands the safety net for the truly needy without increases in cost?

RENAISSANCE also predicted that illicit drug trafficking as a large-scale enterprise would vanish in a very short period of time as the controls tightened. The ability to make money selling illegal drugs would cease to exist–no anonymous paper currency, no medium of exchange, no sale. Large-scale casual use of illicit drugs would cease almost as soon as retail supplies were consumed. Although demand would remain high, the loss of paper currency would eliminate the funding. Drug trafficking after all was a retail business.

Some users would continue to produce small amounts of product via home labs and basement gardens. Barter exchange would continue to provide product to a diminished market base, but the economic and political clout of the industry would be broken.attempts to suborn the pharmaceutical industry would also fail.While abuse of prescription drugs was expected to surge in the short term, the medical community by and large would support rather than oppose the effort to eliminate drug abuse. Fraudulent prescription writing for profit was no less penetrable than other illegal drug trafficking operations. In the end, the profit motive would be found lacking.

Organized crime operations in legitimate as well as illegal businesses would be identified and exterminated as well. At the low-tech end of the scale the first casualties would be common street gangs. Deprived of product, sales, profits and customers, the gangs would first splinter and eventually, dissolve.

All aspects of government business whether local, state or federal, to include campaign financing, would be discouraged from involvement in illicit transactions simply due to the lack of anonymous printed currency as a medium of exchange. In fact, all criminal activity would have to move offshore to rapidly shrinking "free trade" zones that still maintained a paper currency.

Trade in gems, precious metals, and high end collectibles as a dodge to avoid the control of financial transactions would wither as the ability to convert the value of these holdings into a medium of exchange other than barter commodity becomes increasingly difficult to achieve.

The Pacific Rim industrializing economies and the newly independent nation of Quebec, would likely be temporarily flooded with organizations and individuals emigrating from the US in an attempt to maintain their holdings and continue their illicit activities. Increased

criminal activity, plus the demonstrated speed and
efficiency of the new "cash-less" economy were expected
to provoke a crisis level response by affected foreign
governments.

Not only would they suffer the negative consequences of
an influx of criminal operations into the free zone trade
areas still issuing and using paper currency, but the
qxuantum leap in US efficiency would threaten their
already declining competitive viability. Bottom line: The
US would emerge as a balanced budget player with an
unassailable cyber-currency in the worlds financial
markets. Eventually, only the most remote and
underdeveloped regions of the globe would continue to
operate with paper currencies. These remaining free trade
zones, havens for economic refugees of the worst type--
criminals mostly--would ultimately be forced to join the
new order.

Thurston had smiled at the memory of President-elect J.
D. Waites nodding again and again, flipping the pages,
punctuating his bobbing head with "uh huh," "yeah," "got
it," doing his patented quick-scan of the folder on his knees.
J.D.'s strength was the ability to retain more on the first
look than most of his peers could digest in hours of review.
Thurston respected that, and truth be told, feared it. J. D.,
for all his charm and magnetism, could be ruthless, even
brutally so, if crossed. Tim checked his day planner again
and called for his car. He had to go schmooze that rat
bastard Cunningham, meet the Speaker of the House, that
rat bastard Cunningham, and one didn't keep the Speaker
waiting.

***

CHAPTER THREE

Scotty's Diner, December 19, 2008
St. Louis, Missouri

Keith Randall was not having a good day. That wasn't news. He hadn't had a good day for quite some time. By night, Keith was a club musician, playing the bass guitar--standards mostly--and despite his unquestionable talent and accomplishment as a musician he barely managed to earn enough to eat and pay the rent. On any given day, he was one gig ahead of being homeless.

Keith had known the thrill of playing stadiums. The "almost" but not closed record deals, opening for the "big acts", the screaming fans lining up for his autograph, the recording studio gigs, brushing so close to success, then seeing others make it to the top, and finally, over the long years, the down sloping, day to day struggle to survive.

Keith was not unacquainted with bad times. "His" music, the great classic rock tunes of his generation were only played now by the diehard "All oldies, all the time" FM stations. Despite years of striving and enthusiastic self-denial, he wasn't a kid anymore and hadn't been for thirty years. High School Class of 1969, working musician since 1967, the glory days had faded long ago... fifty-six years old and still picking. *Well, shit, until last night he could still hope to be like Willie Nelson. Willie didn't hit the big time until he was so old he looked like hell before breakfast.* It would help if he liked country music. Unfortunately, Keith hated country music. He hated playing country for people who liked it even more.

The worthy young lady seated across from Keith, Chris Rose, Officer Chris Rose, of the St. Louis Police Department, shared Keith's musical sentiments wholeheartedly. Twenty years younger than Keith, Chris believed the only music worth listening to had been recorded before she was born. Keith's tales of the era of real "rock and roll" and life "on the road" fascinated Chris and it seemed she couldn't get enough. She loved to get Keith talking, to regale her by the hour with stories of the "great" and "near great" of that era. Keith had personally known many of them. Some of them had even been counted among his closest friends. Most of them were retired now–or dead. In an earlier time Chris probably would have been a "groupie," attaching herself to one band or another.

The fact was, the musical groups of that era were long gone and there was no one left to be a groupie for. There was more to their friendship than music. Keith and Chris besides being lovers, were fellow travelers in a movement that had first gained notoriety in the 1990's. They were both drilling members of the Missouri Minutemen. They had met at a Minutemen-sponsored shooting match. Keith had placed well in the assault rifle competition with his Chinese-made SKS.

Keith had known for some time that due to his membership in the Missouri Minuteman his life had come under close scrutiny. He often felt but could not locate who was watching him. At odd times his phone would make strange clicking noises when he lifted the receiver to place a call. His garbage had often been picked up hours before the truck picked up his neighbor's garbage.

Lately, Keith had taken to mocking the watchful strangers. Occasionally, he would pick up the phone and announce he was going out for coffee and offer to pick up donuts for "the boys." Sometimes, if he had been drinking, he would get worked up into a rage and bellow obscenities for the benefit of anyone listening via the electronic bugs he was convinced were recording his every utterance. Mostly he just sulked and hated.

Chris had heard Keith's suspicions before and believed she might also have reason to be concerned. She also knew that Keith's inability to locate and confront his tormentors was slowly driving him more than a little crazy.

Until last night ... Chris listened as Keith leaned forward, his eyes burning with triumph, despite the bad day he was having. "Last night I caught one."

Chris glanced at the other tables watching for a quick head movement or raised newspaper that would reveal an unusual interest in their conversation from the other patrons.

Keith leaned back, "I left for my gig last night, and when I got there, the owner had decided he didn't need a band, so he just told us to get our shit and leave! Can you believe that asshole? So I load up my shit–my guitar case was stolen by the way–Jesus I hate these redneck bars, so, all my shit's in the car, I get three blocks away from home and my front tire blows. So here I am, my car full of shit I had to bring back from the gig, flat tire, no money and I'm ready to kill the first asshole that looks sideways at me. Anyway, I walk around the corner of my house, and some asshole's coming out the front door. The bastard was in my house Chris!"

Keith looked around and dropped his voice "the piece of shit never even saw me, he was dickin' around with some electronic bullshit, I didn't really see what it was, it was dark as shit, and I wasn't really thinking that rationally by then. So anyway, I've got my fretless bass in my hand–I wasn't gonna leave my fretless sittin' in the car, not in my neighborhood–so, I just kinda raised it up and brought the head stock down on the son of a bitch's head. He dropped like a rock. He didn't even move."

"I wasn't sure if he was dead or what, so I'm standing there looking at him wondering what to do, when the little prick starts moaning. So I reached down and got a hold of his arms, and pulled him across the yard to the driveway and kind of dragged him down to the street. I just left him there on the curb. For all I know he's still there. I haven't been back. I've been up all night. I waited until this morning and called you. So that was my night. How was yours?"

Chris looked down at her hands 'boring compared to yours...' "I wondered why you weren't answering the phone last night. I had stopped by that shit hole bar so I knew you weren't playing there." Chris looked at Keith's face and realized how bad this was gonna be. She could at least get him out of town.

"Look Keith, I didn't hear anything about this last night, and I worked until this morning. Whoever you smacked must not have had a back up. All in all, I'd say you're damn lucky to be here. Keith, you gotta leave for a while."

Chris opened her purse and pulled out some crumpled bills. She had less than a hundred dollars. She grabbed his hands and put the money in them, "you have to leave now Keith. Don't try to contact me or anyone else. Let me see if I can sort this out. I'll leave word with your father in Tennessee when I have something for you. For God's sake don't use any credit cards. If they're looking for you it's the first trace they'll use."

Keith tried to think, and found he couldn't. This wasn't what he wanted. He knew that. The money in his hand didn't have much future either.

Keith stood up, "I guess this is it Chris, I'm sorry. I don't regret what I did but I sure hate to leave." Chris just squeezed his hand, "Go on now Keith, hurry, just go and don't stop. Go now!"

The waitress found a nice tip but no customers. The busboy clearing the table informed her that the lady had just left.

"She looked like she was crying or something."

***

December 19, 2008
South Beach
Miami/Dade County, Florida

The strap from her bag was actually cutting a groove into the skin on her bare shoulder. Her high-heeled sandals were performing the same service on her feet. It was better now that the bag was only half full.

Ana Rodriguez was a busy little "Smurf" today. "Smurfs" were money launderers who, like the cartoon characters, worked all day scurrying from one bank to another and depositing cash for their masters. She ought to be busy. To the banks she patronized, Ana was a successful young entrepreneur with literally hundreds of thriving businesses. Business was booming. Miami was a happening place.

Each year, Federal Reserve Member Banks all over the country would run a slight deficit in cash reserves that the Federal Reserve System would alleviate by providing additional currency through one of the 12 Federal Reserve Regional banks. Miami typically posted a two or three billion-dollar surplus. The hard work of couriers like Ana, "Smurfs" in the parlance of the trade, ensured this would always be so.

Ana's job description was simple–take a bag stuffed with currency and make deposits all over the city in as many accounts as required to stay off the CTR radar screen. CTRs were currency transaction reports. CTRs were required for any deposit in excess of $9,999.99. The way to avoid unwanted attention resulting in filing a CTR was to limit the amount of the deposit to around $8,000.00.

Ana deposited hundreds of thousands of dollars a week. For this, Ana was well paid. As a bonus, she could have as much "product" as she liked and she wouldn't have to worry about having nice clothes to wear. It beat the shit out of hooking for a living, no pimps, no johns, no cops. She even found she enjoyed the small talk with the tellers. Sometimes she would daydream that she really did own a little boutique or café or gift shop in the city. So long as the tellers did not question her too closely, she could even enjoy making up funny little stories about her customers or the landlord, or some new product line she hoped to get. It was all very pleasant once you got used to it.

At first she had been terrified to enter a bank and attempt to deposit the drug money. She had slowly realized that the banks were more than willing to accommodate new depositors and would do so with a smile.

"Just don't push the envelope Ana," her boss had told her. "Look and act like what you are claiming to be. You are a small businesswoman with a large cash flow."

"Don't act like a fool and you will be treated as a valued customer. Bankers are *putas*–whores Ana, no different than you used to be. Did you ever turn down a customer with cash Chiquita? No? See, what I am saying is true, is it not?"

Ana was not a fool. She did well and was rewarded with more deposits to make. Some organizations attempted to use peasants; illiterate, ragged fools to launder money at check cashing outlets and money order stores. Ana was grateful she did not work with such low life fools, and, she was smart enough to not even think about running off with a full bag of cash. Ana knew that eventually, soon in fact, the wads of bills in her bag would no longer be of any value. '*Worrying about it will not change it*' she stoutly reminded herself.

She adjusted the strap cutting into her shoulder and entered the lobby of one of her favorite banks. The whoosh of the climate controlled, artificially chilled air rushing through the opening felt almost as if she had passed beneath a fountain, cool waters spilling over her and beyond into the hot concrete and asphalt of the city.

Smiling brightly, she crossed the marble lobby, heels clicking smartly on the polished surface. This really was her favorite bank. So nice inside, it was truly beautiful, a lovely cathedral filled with money.

***

CHAPTER FOUR

December 22, 2008
Boston, MA

John O'dea awoke fuzzy headed from too much wine the previous evening. Dawn was up early fretting over Christmas, what dishes to prepare and when to serve, and even those last minute gifts. Her attention to detail at least for now, would be as much hindrance as help. Time was flying. The promise of fresh coffee penetrated the thicket that was encasing his brain.

The local news had run a series of "human interest" stories showcasing the imminent transfer to a paperless national currency. The stories were done with a light touch, stressing the humor of the situation by occasionally inserting clips from the old Star Trek films where naturally, money had not existed in the United Federation of Planets for hundreds of years. John had padded into the kitchen barefoot and slipping his arms around Dawn said, "what's on the tube?" Dawn laughed and reached for the coffeepot and began to fill a mug for John. "Watch it paddy boy; I'm armed." She handed him the mug and the remote. "Turn it up, I wasn't really listening."

As the audio came up, the news anchor was leading into a sound bite from a woman who had just finished purchasing several items from one of the giant, consumer electronics chain stores: computer games for her son, a new video camera unit for their home computer, and of course, a matching unit for her sister.

"I couldn't believe how fast they were moving." The camera panned to the clerks while the shopper described the speed with which her "purchases," had been scanned totaled, bagged, and paid for.

It was true. There were three different types of registers for three different types of payment. The most familiar type, for cash, credit card and check payments seemed to be moving in slow motion.

The queues were moving more briskly at the register line for CyCred card payments. CyCred "card holders" were using digital cash but the verification procedures, swiping the card through a reader, and then punching up verification codes, still took some time to complete.

The queues at the "BIOCHEK" line were moving at almost walking speed through the process. Scans for either hand or forehead were completed in less than a blink of the eye. As quickly as the bar codes were scanned for every purchase the tax was tallied and the BIOCHEK transaction cleared through the individual's bank. Three clerks were engaged at the end of this line bagging up purchases as fast as they could to prevent a bottleneck from forming.

Christmas music closed the piece as the anchor turned back to face the camera. In the background an old woman in the cash and check line was slowly counting out bills and coins for her purchase while customers in line behind her shifted their packages and rolled their eyes.

"Technology seems to be bringing at least "some shoppers" a measure of Christmas cheer–and now, if you're having second thoughts about that special gift...."

John flipped the station to mute. The thought of being herded along in a crowded mall shriveled his resolve to get out and finish his own shopping. He would gladly pay for someone to do it for him.

Dawn leaned over and gave him a peck on the cheek, reading his thoughts exactly.

"I have an idea John, let's use the limo, and we'll go out together, and we'll both get our shopping done, and afterwards we can stretch out at home and pretend it never happened."

John stood and arched his back yawning, "You got a deal Darlin, I'll be right with you." John was humming a Christmas Carole as he headed for the shower.

***

CHAPTER FIVE

December 22, 2008
Southwest Renaissance Center
Gallup, New Mexico

'*Seventeen dollars an hour and full benefits too.*' Alan dipped his swab and wrung the water before reapplying it to the tile. This was a hell of a big complex. By the time Alan had completed the 10th floor of just this wing he could expect to start all over again on the 1st floor. It was that big.

Alan remembered his Dad telling him about painting the Golden Gate Bridge. They would start at one end and when they had painted all the way to the other end, other workers had already started painting a new coat back at the other end. A perpetual motion painting machine. *'Of course that was just a bridge,'* Alan thought.

Alan wasn't really an inmate. He was sort of a trustee. Alan had been "processed" through a "beta site" Renaissance Center in Alabama. He had been twenty-seven years old and doing time in a medium security Federal Prison in Huntsville. Federal because he was caught with a half ounce of cocaine. The punishment for distribution of cocaine and other narcotics had been ratcheting up throughout the 1990's. By comparison, in terms of length of sentencing and parole opportunities, Second Degree Manslaughter was quite often treated as a less serious offense than narcotics trafficking.

Alan felt lucky to be here. The pay wasn't great but they left him alone and he got plenty to eat. Soon he would have lots of company. Southwest was designed to process 100,000 "clients" annually. It resembled a university campus with wings of dormitories, auditoriums, sports facilities and classrooms. At the center of the campus there was a super-modern, medical facility.

Alan had been doing "good time" inside the Huntsville Alabama Federal Prison. Alan was dependable. Sometimes, for a nominal fee, he would obtain a little bit of contraband for a fellow inmate, say a joint or two or maybe a pint of Jack Daniel's whiskey. He filled a need. The guards tried to look the other way and the more predatory inmates left him alone.

They had brought Alan down to see a visitor from Washington who wanted to interview selected prisoners for possible transfer to a new type of facility. The dude waiting for him was completely cool, he saw that right off. He had offered his hand to shake and motioned Alan to sit with him for a few minutes to "get acquainted." *'That was so smooth, that was "smoove" with a capital "V."'* He had said his name was "Jerry Carpenter" and that he had looked forward to meeting him. He had asked Alan if he was getting along okay given that Alan was doing time in prison and all that. Alan had mumbled something to the effect it wasn't so bad if you didn't think about shit too much.

Despite Alan's less than coherent response, Jerry seemed to really be listening to what Alan had to say. It was like Jerry really wanted to understand what you were thinking and feeling and hoping, *'kind of scary, but nice'.*

Then Jerry says he has some ideas about how things could be better for people who were having a hard time, and would Alan be interested? For half a second Alan thought, *'shit, here it comes, the dude's just a slick talking "butt monkey."'*

But it wasn't that at all. Jerry just starting talking this really deep shit about the world changing and how things worked changing and "reality" changing, and like how things were going to be really different, really soon and a lot of people were gonna have to make some really big changes, or they just flat weren't gonna make it. Jerry didn't want to see anyone not make it.

Then he had looked at Alan, (a dope dealer and not a very good one!), like he was counting on him to fix all the problems and said "Alan, we need you to help us out on this. We have a lot of work and we need smart people like you to get it rolling. I promise you won't regret it if you decide to join us. I can get you out of here Alan."

Before he could be transferred,The prison infirmary would have to do a complete work-up,physical exam,blood tests, eye test, urine and stool specimens, the whole gamut would be run. Jerry explained it was standard procedure. Alan didn't mind. The infirmary was not unpleasant and they even had some fine looking female nurses temporarily assigned to the ward to facilitate processing the new selectees.

In the process of drawing blood, DNA would be analyzed and recorded digitally on a small device, no larger than a grain of rice.When fully loaded,the device would contain Alan's genetic history, along with retinal scan features, facial thermography and other precise measurements of his facial features and of course a digital map of Alan's fingerprints. The device would, when interrogated electronically, transmit any of the data recorded within, to identify, locate, or download the medical history of its host. Once injected into the tissues of Alan's forearm it was virtually undetectable. Any attempt,by Alan or anyone other than an approved facility, to remove or modify the device would generate a digitally encoded transmission that would lead authorities to the location of the device.

Then,in a painless procedure that took less than a second to complete for each,micro tattoos were applied to Alan's forehead and the backs of his hands. The tattoos were not visible in ordinary light and required a simple, ultraviolet spectrum laser reader to scan the code. Alan was not even aware he had been injected and branded.

Two weeks later Alan was on a bus with U. S. Marshall Casey Maclin heading for Muscle Shoals,Alabama. Jerry was waiting for him when he arrived. He had turned to the Marshall and said "you can take the cuffs with you Marshall,Alan won't need them here."

Jerry shook Alan's hand, "let's go meet the rest of the team" and led Alan through the gate of the compound.

Alan remembered brightly lit passageways and a lot of people moving back and forth, carrying clipboards and briefcases and pushing carts, like a hospital but different. He was led into a small auditorium that, like the passageway, was crowded with people. There was a sea of strangers here, talking and nodding their heads, shaking hands and forming into little groups and then breaking off to greet or meet some other arrival. He saw uniforms too.

Jerry said "grab a seat, I'll catch up to you later" and just left him standing there, no handcuffs, no guards, free to bolt if he wanted too. Alan sat down. Then, there was a low rumble that died off as everyone took seats. The lights dimmed and an overhead screen the length of the stage lit up and soft music began to play. Jerry stepped out on the stage and walked over to a podium set off to one side.

Jerry surveyed the room, smiling and nodding to those in the front and waving to some seated further toward the back of the auditorium. Somewhere from the middle rows of the hall a few handclaps of applause began and immediately everyone in the room joined in. 'The dude was so cool.' He just laughed and made a "what, for me?" gesture and joined in, applauding the audience for applauding him.

'What _is_ this?' Alan had looked around but saw only good cheer and smiling faces.

The applause swelled up and then died off just right, naturally as if on cue. "What an inspiration it is to be right even if it's just once in a lifetime."

Jerry had carried it off in such a way that everyone started laughing and clapping all over again. When the room grew still again, Jerry started talking. Alan had really listened and he could still remember every word.

"Some of the folks in this room tonight have been with "RENAISSANCE" from the beginning, and some of you have been here for about five minutes."

Alan looked around to see if anyone was looking at him and saw that there were a few curious but not unfriendly glances his way.

"I want all of you to know that you're here because we wanted you here. We hope you'll stay because you want to stay. I believe you will find no better proposition in this world than the proposition we offer here."

"What we offer is victory, a new life, and a reawakening of the unlimited possibilities of the human spirit. I want to tell you all about it. I am anxious for you to hear what RENAISSANCE is going to be. We will begin tomorrow."

"For our new colleagues, we have paired you off with 'running mates'. Your 'running mates', if you haven't already met yours, are here to help you. If you will give us a moment to get organized following the meeting, they will help you with your quarters and see to any of your needs before turning in for the night. For now, just relax, get settled in, and rest easy."

Then Jerry had looked right at Alan, "I assure you, you are among friends."

"Dexter Kershaw," Alan's "running mate," had walked up to him when the lights came back up.

"Hey Alan, I'm Dexter." They shook hands. "Let's get out of here. Are you hungry?"

Dexter was steering him out of the commotion in the auditorium. He seemed to know a lot of the people and stopped often to shake hands and make introductions. Alan felt like a new kid at school. Finally, they were back in the passageway.

"Sorry about that Alan, you'll get used to it. We'll be leaving here soon. Until we get our assignments, things will be a little tight."

They rode down a spacious two-way escalator and turned left in the lobby and passed through a pair of automatic doors. Alan could smell food now. It smelled like real food, not "prison" food.

Then past a sign, "COMMISSARY" and through a glass and chrome revolving door, and the full force of the delicious aroma hit them. Dexter handed Alan a tray, "I'm starved Alan, how about you?"

Alan looked around at the incredible sight of golden fried crispy chicken, tray after tray of vegetables and pasta dishes, baked potatoes, fries, mashed potatoes, stir fried beef and pork, fried shrimp, salads, and mounds of fresh fruits, whole and sliced, everything arranged just like a fancy restaurant would. A little knot in his stomach loosened.

Dexter nudged him with his tray and grinned, "Hey man, you gonna eat or what?"

Alan had smiled for the first time. He grabbed for the silverware and stepped up to the line, "let's do it Dexter."

***

December 24, 2008
IPTF HQ
Washington, D.C.

Christmas music played softly over the acoustic masking system that IPTF had installed to thwart attempts to covertly listen into the conversations in the various conference and work areas of the complex. Utilizing transducers attached to the surfaces of walls throughout the building, the music had a ghostly quality and usually, one barely noticed the sound, but if you placed your ear, or any other device to the wall, it would sound like you had put headphones on and cranked the volume up to the point of pain.

The staff of IPTF, from low-level technicians and clerical personnel to the top administrators and deputies, had accepted the loss of the traditional Christmas work schedule. While other agencies were enjoying the usual holiday season of working a half-day at most, not to mention the hordes of government employees who were vacationing and spending time with their families, the IPTF was working twelve hour shifts.

Jerry Carpenter had consoled his own family by reminding them it was just this once, it couldn't be helped and that next year it would be different.

As Jerry reviewed the reports in front of him, he wondered if that assessment might not be a little optimistic. There was so much to be done. He literally felt squeezed by the rush of events. He knew what had been accomplished and felt justifiably proud of what he and his team had achieved. The Director of the IPTF, the Honorable Tim Thurston, Captain, USN(Retired), had said as much, adding that the President was not unaware of his performance. Secretly, Jerry could give a shit what

Thurston thought of him or of anything else. Thurston was a lickspittle lapdog. At least he had been able to run RENAISSANCE the way he wanted to and that was what mattered.

Back in 1989, Jerry had done a research paper on a Federal Detention Facility in Marion, Illinois. It was ironic on a cosmic scale. The Warden, an ardent antismoker, had eliminated smoking privileges for both the staff and the inmate population. The Warden had been completely oblivious as to any potential outcome to his petty act of social engineering. He knew it would be unpopular of course. Compliance would take some time to effectively achieve. But, smoking was evil and dirty and the smell of tobacco made him physically ill. The unintended consequences had fascinated Jerry and he had obtained permission to take a leave of absence from his Masters Program at the University of Illinois, Dekalb to visit the prison and study the phenomena.

He had come across the article while waiting for a turn at the card files in the University's main library and amusing himself by leafing through a popular, national weekly News Magazine. The article was just a half-column under the heading "Across the Nation." It turns out that more than just olfactory offense to the Good Warden had been reduced. Jerry had read and reread the short article. *Some petty, bureaucratic son of a bitch, with the unquestioned authority of a Prison Warden to do as he wished, had unintentionally discovered something of unprecedented magnitude. Not only was he unaware of the implications of the results of his actions, but apparently the writer, whoever he or she was, as well as, the editor and publisher of the magazine, were each, as equally dull witted.*

He had carefully torn the article off the page and folded it into his pocket. When his turn came to use the card files,

Jerry had stared blankly for a moment and turning on his heel, headed back to his apartment to write a letter to the Dean outlining his ideas. A week later armed with a letter of introduction from the Dean he arrived in Marion and began to work.

The prison population at Marion, like all prisons, was a fully functioning society with a unique microeconomy. Denied by prison regulations to receive or hold cash money, they were issued a line of credit each month worth $40.00 that allowed them to purchase - from the prison exchange, a variety of small items; toiletries, approved paperbacks, limited choices of candy and chewing gum, and of course, cigarettes.

Cigarettes were the coin of the realm for a society lacking a universal, anonymous unit of cash currency. Brands were valued according to personal taste, the most universally acceptable brand, defined the, "gold standard," in relative value. Three packs of a less valuable brand as measured by the aggregate tastes of the prison population might equal only two packs of the gold standard" brand. Even nonsmokers traded in the coin of the realm. Although they found that the smoking population would always demand a discount for their end of any transaction with them, the smoker's reasoning being that the nonsmokers had an unfair advantage in that they were not compelled by habit to consume their own assets. Transactions, for drugs, sex, homemade weapons, pornography, "protection," prized work assignments, and even beatings and murder, could be financed with tobacco. Loans with interest were common.

At the end of the month, before new credits at the prison exchange would be available, common personal items needed were always available from certain inmates for a price computed in cigarettes. If an inmate had smoked or spent his cigarettes, he could arrange a loan at interest to be repaid to the inmate "banker" or "merchant" when new credits were issued at the beginning of the next month. Inmates who specialized in these operations themselves paid other inmates in the coin of the realm for protection, as well as, to enforce, if need be, the terms of the loans.

Prior to the ban, as Jerry's paper explained, a recurring monthly, "business cycle," had existed in which the supply of, "currency," within the system rose and fell. As the supply of cigarettes in, "circulation," were consumed by the smoking population, the value of the, "currency," rose due to increasing scarcity. At the end of the month, "M1" or "C1," more accurately, the measure of cigarettes in circulation, was at its lowest point in the cycle. Then the cycle would begin anew at the beginning of the next month with the issuance of new credit from the prison exchange. The inmates would spend their credits on cigarettes and the currency would temporarily re-inflate as the supply of cigarettes in circulation was restored. Of course, arbitrage and speculation of a sort would occur.

However, the clockwork regularity of the monthly business cycle limited the profits by limiting the absolute range and rate of change in value. In the last few days before new credits were issued to the inmates, prices for goods and services as computed in cigarettes, would begin to stabilize and even rise in anticipation of the new month bringing a fresh infusion of , "capital," (cigarettes). Additionally, the cycle was also somewhat flattened by the regular introduction of cigarettes arriving via packages mailed to the inmates by family and friends who understood the economies of prison life and who were not allowed to send cash in any event.

Basic economic theory amply demonstrated and predicted all the above. Simple lessons of supply and demand, or the inflation or deflation of money supplies was not what intrigued Jerry. It was what happened when the "money" supply was eliminated. It was not credits for the inmates to purchase the few things offered at the prison store that were eliminated. They still received the same amount in credit, the equivalent of $40.00 per month. Unfortunately, they could not spend this credit anywhere but in the store. They could not trade their credit at the store to any other inmate or prison employee, but they had been able to convert their credit to a universally accepted anonymous currency–cigarettes. Yes, prior to the elimination of cigarettes, Marion Federal Detention Center had a robust microeconomy fueled by an adequate supply of anonymous, universally accepted, unit of exchange, just like the cash economy of the larger society outside the walls. The anonymity of the "coin of the realm" inside the walls had facilitated and financed a wide array of criminal activity.

There were two factors at work Jerry reasoned. The first was that permitted purchases were only available via a non-cash system of credits and debits. No "script," no transferable, tangible store of value, just a ledger account with a recurring infusion of $40.00 each month that the inmate could "spend," but only in the store, and he could only buy what was permitted. What was offered in the store was all that was permitted. Cigarettes were the only convertible, transferable store of value. They didn't spoil–although a smoker would prefer a fresh unopened pack, they could be exchanged in units of any number, singly, five, ten, fifteen or a full package of twenty. Additionally, for larger purchases or transactions, trading individual packs in multiples up to a full carton of ten could be negotiated. Multiple carton transactions were rare and almost always were used to fund purely criminal and violent transactions: physical beatings of other inmates, or outright murder.

The term microeconomy was descriptive both of the tiny population it served, less than 3,000 inmates and of the actual value of the currency in circulation. If an inmate spent just a dollar a day on anything other than cigarettes, he would only be able to afford one carton of cigarettes per month. That worked out to about a third of a pack of cigarettes per day. Engaging in smuggling of contraband, liquor, drugs, and, providing services, sex, "protection", revenge or enforcement beatings, selling of favors, and even murder for hire, all of which could earn one "currency," appreciably augmented the inmates "disposable income."

Unfortunately for the prison system, these activities and behaviors were not only undesirable, they tended to reinforce the antisocial tendencies that had led to the incarceration of the inmates to begin with. For those inmates lacking contact with the outside world to send them permitted items, candy bars, or cigarettes (both were permitted only in small amounts-10 bars of candy/one carton of cigarettes per package, per month), there were no other options available.

To Jerry this was the ultimate paradox. You create a prison to house and contain individuals for the purpose of eliminating the impact of their actions and behaviors on society at large. Then, you realize that even within this prison society where there are no rights - only rules and punishment, criminality still flourished. In fact, the behaviors that caused society to incarcerate them appeared to be their only hope of survival inside the walls.

'How could this be'? Rules couldn't break the cycle. Even locking them up and reducing simple human needs, such as permission to use the bathroom, to a privilege to be earned, could not change these men and women. 'What was the root problem? What name would you give it?

What was crime and what was simple survival? If it was simple survival inside the prison system, what appreciable difference was there outside the walls where choices for so many seemed to be just as limited?'

'All crime is retail'. Jerry looked at what he had written. Then he had read it aloud, sitting at a scarred bureau he used for a typing table. "All crime is retail."

Alone in his room in a cheap boarding house in Marion, Illinois, he had shouted it, "ALL CRIME IS RETAIL!" What the Warden had done at Marion Federal Penitentiary was simple. That he hadn't a clue to its full meaning did not concern Jerry.

Here is what happened. When cigarettes were removed from the prison exchange system, a deflationary "financial crisis" engulfed the inmate population's economy. Despite attempts to hide, hoard and smuggle cigarettes, despite attempts to find places to light up without being discovered, the use and possession of cigarettes either as a unit of currency or for personal consumption was, over time, utterly eliminated. At first it was business as usual, and the currency became exponentially more valuable. A single cigarette eventually commanding the value of an entire pack before the ban took place.

It was a time of danger for both guard and inmate. Withdrawal symptoms among the smokers were adding an edge to what was already a potentially explosive atmosphere in the best of times. Marion was a maximum-security facility. It was "hard time" for maximum offenders doing the maximum term. Life sentences were considered good fortune, if parole was still a remote possibility.

Many had either been sentenced to life without parole or had so many life sentences piled end to end that parole was still possible theoretically but few people expected to live 120 years.

Confiscation and removal of the few privileges or personal belongings permitted, began in earnest. Many guards quit. Most were smokers but some just quit out of disgust or fear of the inmate population's potentially violent response to the new policy.

'They should have stayed' Jerry thought. The inmates still had their credits for monthly purchases, and although a "Snickers bar" might be a nice gesture or even a quid pro quo for a favor granted, it would never become a replacement for cigarettes as a durable, scalable and universally accepted form of currency with which to negotiate the exchange of goods and services.

Within just a few months of barring tobacco-all tobacco, the incidence of criminal activity dropped off dramatically. A pack of cigarettes casually traded for say an act of sex, or a carton for one, loosely-rolled, marijuana joint was no longer possible. Not that the inmates wouldn't have desired to obtain these little comforts, there simply was no profit motive for the vendor. Every criminal act ever engaged in for profit began to first decline and then stop all together.

Violent inmates still beat, raped and murdered if that was their predilection and they were sufficiently provoked. Violence for the sake of violence and rape for the sake of rape would continue, but the opportunity to profit by brokering for, or providing protection from, such activities no longer existed. Drugs such as marijuana and cocaine had always been scarce commodities inside the prison and they became infinitely more so after the ban.

Jerry Carpenter felt he was on to something much larger than Marion Federal Penitentiary. The paper practically wrote itself and to his surprise and pleasure was reprinted in a number of scholarly and legal periodicals. A phone call by the Bush administration inviting him to take part in a "Blue Ribbon" commission on Criminal Justice Reform led to a series of official and quasi-official assignments of increasing visibility and responsibility. Jerry served with distinction in both the Bush and Clinton administrations, culminating in what was now a sub-cabinet level appointment, Assistant Deputy Director of the IPTF, executing the office of RENAISSANCE Program Manager.

The music played on. Jerry sat alone and penciled revisions, a dull ache in his lower back spreading to his legs, 'so much to do, so little time'.

***

CHAPTER SIX

December 25, 2008
Soddy Daisy, TN

Keith hoped he would be welcome dropping in on Christmas day. He had known Art and his family for more years than he cared to count-since before they had children and they were all grown and flown from the nest. The adrenaline rush of whacking that agent or whatever the hell he was and then fleeing St. Louis was long gone. Keith was tired and hungry and knew that he looked like shit and probably smelled worse.

He had been living in his car about half the time, hiding out with friends he trusted when he could. The first three days he had slept in his car at truck stops along I-24. He had driven half way to Chicago but the cold and uncertainty of what he would do when he got there turned him back. One day he had just driven along secondary roads through quiet little towns in Kentucky. As a musician, he had played in some of them. Most of all he would feel how alone he suddenly was. It was too much. After two nights in Nashville, and one night in Pigeon Forge and last night Keith pulled off the road in Soddy Daisy about a half mile from Art Chandler's place and waited for morning.

No doubt about it, it was getting cold. Keith stamped his feet. He could see his reflection in the glass of the storm door. The rippled glass was not flattering. He ran his hand through his hair, greasy and lank from the road and too little sleep.

The door opened and there stood Art just beaming with pleasure "Good Lord, Keith Randall, you get in here you big old thing! Betty, we got a Christmas bear come to visit!" Keith towered in the doorway six feet four inches even slumped over and haggard. Betty appeared and gave him a hug before Keith could say, "I wouldn't - I haven't had a shower for a while." Art took Keith's coat, "You look like you been up all night."

Keith had moved to the fireplace and turned to warm his backside, "My man it feels like I've been up for a week. I hate to just drop in like this." Art cut him off, "hush now Keith you don't need no 'invite' here. How's your Dad doin'?"

Keith closed his eyes and hung his head, " I don't know Art, haven't talked to him or anyone for quite a while. I guess he's fine." Betty glanced at Art "I've got some coffee ready let me just get some." Art followed her into the kitchen and went to the refrigerator to get out some butter and jelly and a basket of homemade rolls leftover from dinner the night before.

"This is a nice surprise Keith. The girls sure would be tickled to see you. David's still in Boston, still rowing and going to school." There was no answer from the living room. Art shrugged at Betty and finished loading the plate with some cheese and apple slices and carried the food back to the living room. Art saw that Keith had collapsed into a chair and literally passed out in front of the fire. He turned and motioned for Betty to come see, "Let him sleep, he's too wired up over something to sleep for long. I got a bad feeling. Don't call his Dad yet. Let's let him tell us what in the world is goin' on first." Keith snored in agreement. It would keep.

***

FEMA Central Region
St. Louis, MO

Special Agent Buffone was going to have a new part in his hair and a few weeks of convalescent leave. There was a concussion and it was serious but he was definitely going to be fine.

Steven Curlew closed the report. They were spread too damn thin. Someone should have hell to pay for this. *'You don't send in people without backup. God damn it, how many times had he warned this was going to happen. At*

*least the freak that hit Buffone had been too rattled to do
more.'*

The Special Agent in Charge, (SAC), for St. Louis, Steven
Curlew, had survived the house cleaning at FEMA when
the Republicans took the Presidency in 2000. Too junior
to be tainted by the previous administration, Steven had
been in the right place at the right time.

One thing he didn't like was the fact that FEMA had been
placed under the IFTP's thumb and it looked like a
permanent deal. Politicians were vengeful-SOB's. All the
Federal agencies had bled bodies the first six months
following the swearing in of the Republican Governor
from Texas as President of the United States. Any official
that even appeared to have been a political appointee
during the eight years of the previous administration had
been dismissed.

FEMA's losses had been IPTF's gain. In fact, since the
signing of Executive Order 13010 in 1996, the
Infrastructure Protection Task Force had grown like a
cancer, metastasizing and invading the executive branch
of government. Terrified of the vulnerability of an
increasingly interconnected, digital electronic national
infrastructure to terrorist attack or natural disaster, the
federal government had kept the IPTF alive.

In 1998, the Attorney General had asked for and gotten a
fifty million dollar budget to establish a permanent
headquarters for the IPTF. In the beginning, each of the
executive branch departments had appointed qualified
specialists to assist in identifying and advising the
President of national infrastructure vulnerabilities and to
recommend strategies to offset or reduce those areas of
concern. Before the IPTF had a headquarters and regional
structure of its own, the Department of Defense had

hosted the IPTF and provided budget and administrative support,"out of hide."

The writing was on the wall for all the federal departments and agencies. In the original document, the IPTF was guaranteed full support and cooperation from every federal agency and department. This became the basis for every power grab by the IPTF from the start. Justice and Defense felt they were legitimately in charge of this upstart organization and resisted cooperating fully until the Y2K debacle hit the nation in full force. Here the absolute requirement for protecting the national infrastructure of the nation was finally realized.

From the financial markets of the nation to the national power grid to international business, the repair of the ravages of Y2K had taken almost two years of "bridging" and wholesale replacement of much of the nations digital infrastructure.

Although the outgoing Democratic administration had considered implementing an executive order for martial law and other extraordinary measures, to include delaying the inauguration of the new chief executive, a quick read of the political tea leaves persuaded the inner circle of the administration otherwise. Washington had breathed a collective sigh of relief when the inauguration was held without delay.

To his lasting credit, the new President had immediately ended the dangerously escalating campaign in the Balkans unconditionally and unilaterally. In retaliation, the Western European Union, (WEU), left NATO, ending the dominance of U.S. leadership in European affairs. The United Kingdom and Canada opted to strengthen ties with the United States and withdrew from the WEU.

Turning his focus to domestic stability and reestablishing respect and trust for the office of the Presidency, the President quietly and permanently squelched any cabinet level resistance to or bureaucratic infighting with the IPTF.

True, the Y2K "bug" had savaged the national infrastructure. It was also true that the administration was not unwilling to milk the crisis for all the power it could.

Congress lined up in lock step in support of the new administration. Within a couple of budget cycles the IPTF was the best funded and most technologically advanced enforcement arm of the federal government with a largely open ended agenda. Even the National Security Agency, historically renowned for its lofty independence when it came to policy and operations, was brought to heel and made to serve.

FEMA, on the other hand, had been slapped around like a red-haired stepchild. Steven had been amazed at how quickly the culture had changed. The IPTF from its inception was exempt from reporting its findings to the public and could meet and discuss issues and withhold their findings and recommendations from public scrutiny as Top Secret. It could and did make policy. The central theme of IPTF policy was that the IPTF was in charge. The IPTF was not going to brook dissent from the other departments of the executive branch or any other source, public or private.

So, Special agent Tom Buffone had spent Christmas in the hospital. Although he was going to be fine, the severity of the concussion he had suffered dictated that he remain under observation while the injury to his skull healed and the swelling of his brain tissue from the trauma induced edema abated.

All because the IPTF demanded more from FEMA than he or any other regional SAC could safely deliver. It was the same story at ATF and the domestic terrorism units of the FBI and Treasury. There were too many organizations and targets to track. Although they were making significant progress, it was at the cost of pushing the envelope of officer safety.

'No matter', Steven knew, every LEA (Law Enforcement Agency) in the country now had one Keith Randall, now a federal fugitive, on their radar screen and Randall would make a blip somewhere. It was just a matter of time. If nothing else, the tracking device they had placed in his vehicle-if he was stupid enough to keep it-would eventually lead them to his location. They had guessed he would head west. Typically, when these militia types had "booked," they would surface somewhere in the outback regions of Arizona, Wyoming, Utah or Idaho. He had ordered activation of the interrogation system of the relay trunked system targeting all routes west via motor vehicle accordingly.

For the last decade, more so in the past two years, as the fear and hatred of the federal government had festered in the political/religious/racial militia organizations, many of the members were simply "opting out" and voting with their feet. When the time came to collect them, it would not hurt that the target area of operations was concentrated where the agencies could work without a huge media presence and do so outside of urban areas. *'They would get this prick Randall too.'* Steven hoped the extradition would be swift.

***

Boston MA,
December 26, 2008

David's thin frame had been filled to near bursting. Even now, the morning after having gorged himself, David was sure he would not feel the need to eat again anytime soon. He had "done himself proud" as his dad would say, amazing both John and Dawn with his appetite. Well, it all tasted great, much better than the crap he was used to and besides, he had absolutely nothing to do all day today.

David groaned and rolled out of bed and headed for the bathroom. John and Dawn were sleeping in too apparently. They had insisted he spend the night with them. David was a little more homesick than he cared to admit. He had accepted the offer without hesitation. His dad had called yesterday with the news that Keith Randall had shown up on Christmas Eve morning and was staying in David's old room.

David had messed around with the drums a bit. He recognized fairly early that he lacked any real talent and the drum kit went by the way of a yard sale many years ago. Keith though, was a legendary figure to David when he was growing up. He had collected everything Keith had ever written and carefully catalogued and rerecorded the music on Compact Discs. *'I hope Keith had a nice day'*, he thought, brushing his teeth and checking his reflection in the mirror. He was still bulged out from dinner. *'Maybe, I'll take a little road trip home. Sure would make my folks happy, spend some time with Keith and my sisters too.'* The Civic could stand getting blown out a little on the highway too.

His dad had been a little cryptic about Keith's arrival and that wasn't like him. His dad would either tell you the whole deal or keep his own counsel. The fact that he seemed to talk around Keith's sudden visit was strange.

David knew his dad was more than a little opposed to the coming changes. His dad had said "David, I'm praying for all of us. I know you don't agree with me about this new money system. I don't want to argue about that. Whatever happens, I just want you to know you can come home." David spat foam into the sink, he wasn't sure anything was, "going to happen." He understood the economics, the technology and the politics. What he couldn't see was the religious slant. Hell, Napoleon, Hitler, Stalin, even as far back as the Roman emperor Nero, the Church had been proclaiming the end of the world and the rise of the anti-Christ. David supposed that there were some very real concerns about individual privacy rights and *yada yada yada*, but this was stuff for conspiracy kooks and ignorant people who didn't understand the benefits of the new system. David hated that his father was one of those who were opposed.

Just last night over coffee and pumpkin cheesecake, David and John and Dawn had discussed all this crap. *'Who knew more about this than the two of them? Hell, Dawn was the lead programmer on the entire project. It was her system for God's sake.'* She didn't seem like an evil threat to David's eternal soul. She was one of the finest and smartest people David had ever known, and John was no slouch either.

David had asked John whether or not he looked to see drug trafficking go away.

John had just laughed, "Fortunately, I got me a rich woman, cause I'm way too old to do something else for a living."

Dawn had leaned over and kissed John, "you think you got yourself a rich woman."

"Seriously Dawn, do you think drugs are going to just go away because we're eliminating paper currency?"

"You'll have to ask Elliot Ness here about that."

Dawn looked back at David, "in all seriousness David, I suspect it will take a while, like six months and then some at a minimum, but yes, I do think illegal narcotics trafficking as an industry will go away."

"That doesn't mean that some people won't attempt to grow their own or even manufacture stuff in little private home labs, but they'll be really hard pressed to find some way to make it pay."

John agreed, "This whole thing is just a retail business David. At the user end of a long chain of people who move the stuff, the street dealer has to make a sale. They don't accept checks or credit cards for payment. They need cash. They need cash to pay their supplier. Their supplier needs cash to pay his supplier and so on. They need anonymous paper cash that can be laundered and hidden without a way to connect it to the deal, whether the deal is a little bag of dope, or 1,000 kilos of cocaine."

David had pressed, "Won't they just find another way around the problem?"

John shrugged, "Can you think of one? I can't , and I've looked at it every way I can think to look at it. It's not just the money. It's the anonymity of the whole structure. The cash these clowns are making has to be collected at the point of sale-one retail transaction at a time. So the buyer offers the dealer a stolen watch or a television set. The dealer still has to pay his supplier. His supplier wants cash. He can't start a used electronics store. He's a dope dealer and he owes money upline. Within the next six months, everybody the dealers, wholesalers and users are going to have to join the new system."

"Even if a dealer could get away with taking digital transactions peer to peer, he will eventually have to have some legitimate purpose for the transaction. The system will recognize there isn't one. How many people at the user end of the scale will fail to see that they are providing an electronic trail that the police will use to arrest them, and the courts will use to convict them. In the end, whatever you do, you have to convert what you have to a universally accepted legal tender, in this case, digital money that is "unlaunderable" and not in the least, anonymous."

"Sounds like you need to be thinking about updating your resume' John."

"Like I said David, I got me a rich woman. When they decide the time is right or when I get tired of showing up for a do-nothing job I'll retire."

David looked at Dawn "How can anyone not think this is good for the country?"

"Because they don't understand I suppose, or they do but maybe they think it's too much information for the government to use responsibly. I certainly can understand that. I know it's going to be pretty tough for some people to accept. I just hope that after the benefits start to appear, that most of them will see the light."

Like maybe my dad?' David was sure his dad never would.
***

Following the breakup of Canada due to the secession of the province of Quebec in the fall of the year 2004, the english-speaking provinces of Canada elected to throw in with the United States and Britain in the new economy.

While the British maintained a separate digital Pound Sterling, the Canadians had opted for complete monetary union with the United States-as had the Australians and New Zealanders.

South Africa, having slouched down the self-destructive path to black majority rule two decades earlier was now mired in a raging civil war.

With no national consensus upon which to build a stable and just government, the power struggle among tribal coalitions both inside and outside the ruling African National Congress Party and the remnant of the Afrikaner and British colonists who had stayed, exploded into open warfare.

As a result, the horn of Africa, once the only economic success story of Africa descended into savage and intractable conflict. The majority of the nation's capital and western educated workers and managers fled before the storm.

The former French Separatists in Quebec had fared rather better. Quebec, with typical contrariness, had refused both the North American Monetary Union between the United States and Canada, Britain, Australia and New Zealand as well as the European Economic Union. Fiercely independent, Quebec conducted its national economy based on the Quebecois Franc-the last paper-based currency in North America. There were no plans now or ever to eliminate the Franc, either as a printed currency or adopt any form of digital currency.

A free trade zone smack in the center of the North American continent with anonymous paper currency was flourishing. For Canada and the United States this was an annoying but manageable provocation.

In fact, the Quebecois capital markets were awash in foreign remittances. Quebec was experiencing a windfall of assets imported along with all manners of criminal organizations desperate to obtain a safe haven for their illicit activities. These international organizations ran the gamut from traditional organized crime to the more recent Russian American gangs from New York and Florida.

Additionally, there were the aggressive commercial tactics of Chinese, Indian and Russian Republic trade missions eager to work hand in hand with their Anglophobic hosts in any number of shady if not outright illicit enterprises to include arms trading and money laundering.

The rampant and growing corruption seemed to matter very little to the Quebec Government. Their people were employed and the small nation was awash in money. Times were good.

South of the border, Americans wishing to avoid enrolling in the "new economy" were willing and eager to sell their properties, whether they be stocks, bonds, or real estate, to Quebec registered holding companies. These corporations were created for the sole purpose of transferring the assets of the foreign stock owners to safe havens under the Quebec National Government.

A wheat farmer in Kansas could sell his operation, crops in the ground, personal property, vehicles and machinery, in short the entire farm, to a Quebecois holding company. The Quebecois holding company would then assume all financial responsibilities for operating the farm.

All sales of the harvest, and all expenses of the operation were transacted in Quebecois Francs. The stock owners in the holding company continued to operate the farm as before. They were now merely employees of the foreign holding company that owned the property lock, stock and barrel.

All assets of value could be converted in this manner. Cash and cash instruments were transferred to the holding companies.

Many nations in the 21st century held varying amounts of US Currency. In order to maintain that store of "hard currency" a foreign nation's central bank would have to exchange its dollar holdings for digital currency and the paper currency would be removed from circulation and destroyed just as it was being destroyed in the United States.

The United States Government guaranteed a one for one exchange rate to the foreign central bank. The foreign central banks did not have to, or desire to, offer the same guarantees for its private customers.

Over a billion dollars worth of American properties and securities was arriving in Quebec monthly. In a nine trillion-dollar economy this was comparatively small potatoes, but not to Ben Gladding.

Actual foreign government held U.S. printed currency and dollar-based reserves worldwide were fairly limited. It was understood that once the cash reserves had been converted into the digital currency at a guaranteed one for one exchange that the flow of paper currency back to the US Treasury would eventually dry up. After all, there was a finite supply of U.S. currency in circulation.

In addition to dollars in circulation, International Banks and Financial Consortiums whether privately formed or under the aegis of international governmental organizations also held enormous debt in dollar-based credit instruments and loans. These would also be exchanged at a one to one rate for digital currency.

The money traders swept in to feed on the carcass of the disappearing dollar. Unlike foreign governments and other international financial institutions and consortiums, individual holders of dollar assets were not offered one to one exchange for conversion, nor were they guaranteed a stable store of value for any other foreign national currencies they might wish to convert to.

Ben Gladding and his colleagues had determined that this "discount" was rightfully the property of the traders who could set rates and outcomes attractive to themselves in tandem with the central banks of foreign countries.

As a result, American capital, privately held in investment instruments, real property and cash, was being deeply discounted by foreign governments willing to participate in fleecing ordinary Americans desperate to avoid enrolling in the "new economy."

Collectibles, precious metals, gems, any and all stores of value were convertible for the holder willing to pay the discount.

The wheat farm in Kansas worth $2.5 million in U.S. Dollars could be acquired via purchase through foreign holding companies for fifty cents on the dollar. There was no shortage of takers. Better to preserve half of ones assets than to lose it all for nonpayment of taxes and the inability to conduct routine financial transactions necessary to the continued operation of the farm.

In exchange for structuring and administrating these holding companies for the benefit of the foreign government, the discount would be shared equally between the traders and the hosting nation.

Ben Gladding was active in every market in which these

terms had been negotiated. In Quebec alone, "Gladding du Quebec LTD" was pocketing $200 million monthly.

The national governments of both the United States and Canada turned a blind eye to the activities of the money traders. In the end, the paper currencies would be destroyed and the "new economy" would be fully capitalized digitally.

It was a given that the foreign holding companies would eventually collapse under their own weight and the devalued assets would be recouped at cents on the dollar.

Failing that, if need be, all foreign held investments could be renationalized with a stroke of the pen.

The victims of the scheme would have no one to blame but themselves.

***

December 27, 2008
Chattanooga, TN

Chris had reached Keith's dad from a payphone near her apartment. She had apologized for what she had to say, but it was very important that Keith know that he had to get rid of his car, ditch it somewhere and get as far away from it as he could.

When Keith's dad had asked "Why in the world would Keith need to get rid of his car?" she had just said, "I'm sorry Mr. Randall, I can't talk now. If you hear from Keith, tell him what I said."

"What's this about?" Keith Randall Senior was left with a dial tone for an answer.

Keith Senior had in fact heard from Keith through his friend Art. He was just walking to the phone to call Art when Chris rang through. He knew from what little Art had told him that his son was in some trouble with the law but Art had said that was all he knew to tell him for now. He had assured the old man that Keith was okay and it didn't appear that there was a lot to worry about and he would be in touch soon. In the meantime it was best if no one knew Keith was staying with Art. Keith Senior trusted Art to be telling him all he could. He just wished he could talk to his son.

Keith Senior looked at the phone now and wondered if he should call Art on it. He did have to pick up a prescription. He could use a pay phone while he was running that little errand. His driving was a sight to behold and the neighbors always gave him a wide berth, but for a man in his early eighties, Keith Senior got around just fine thank you.

The car started up on the first crank. A 1989 Buick "Le Sabre," it had a few glitches now but it still purred smooth and silky. Keith Senior backed out of the long gravel driveway,' *They can bury me in this car if they like, I guess we're both just about used up.'*

***

The Washington Post
New Years Eve, 2008

Katie Stoner was elated. The Post was the leading source for indepth reporting of the birth of a new age of digital currency. Her sources in and close to the government had trumped both the New York Times and Wall Street Journal. She had worked harder for this than she had ever worked before.

Her approach had been part story telling with nimble and subtle nuances of the "human interest" element, part objective pro and con analysis, and part spin, although she would have firmly rejected any notion that she, Katie Stoner, had been rolled repeatedly by the government. Katie considered herself to be a fiscal conservative, which allowed her ready access to the Republican Party dominated executive and legislative branches of government, and a social progressive that gave her entrée to the leadership of the Democratic minority. In this, Katie was not unlike many in her profession.

The old style liberalism of the post-war era had withered and atrophied since the late 1990's. By the end of the first two Republican administrations controlling the White House as well as both houses of Congress, the new paradigm of American political life had slowly transformed the media as well. The old liberal media "elite" were no longer in charge.

Politics is a vengeful bitch. Unforgiving, and never forgetting, the dominant party had at last stopped behaving like a beleaguered minority and had begun to systematically reward and punish the media according to their support for its agenda. After all, the purpose of any bureaucracy, in truth, is to punish its enemies and reward it's friends.

The Democratic Party had wielded power for almost fifty years and knew the game well. The Republicans perhaps learnt more slowly, but over time, they had honed the cutting edge of political power to a razor sharp instrument.

A time line for implementing digital currency was available to anyone with the time to pore over the multitude of legislation passed by the Congress over the past decade or so. Most interested parties to include members of Congress relied on staff summaries provided by their congressional staffs and by the army of lobbyists lurking in the corridors of the federal government.

Some lobbyists, especially defense and advanced computing and information industries, not only prepared the "executive summaries" they actually briefed senior congressional staffers and their increasingly disconnected bosses.

The sheer scale and complexity of governance and regulation in a global economy were simply beyond the level of competency of any one individual no matter how well prepared and competent. As a result, bills were proposed, "staffed" and passed, the members of Congress more or less conversant with the particulars of the bill he or she voted into law, only to the extent of what they had been told the bill was supposed to accomplish.

The news media, driven by a twenty-four hour news cycle, and needing to retain credibility, lacked the critical eye as well as the time and resources to evaluate what the legislation really intended and what the details revealed as to its implementation. In short, it was too hard.

Katie was a rising media star. It was the most exciting of times. Every day brought new revelations and new statistics that drove the breathless punditry. Katie had talent. She was attractive, articulate and photogenic, especially on television. As a social progressive her bona fides were impeccable. As a fiscal conservative, her diatribes against government waste resonated with clarity and purpose with the American public. Men desired her and women admired her. She was at the top of her game.

This, the last gasp of money as man had defined money since the beginning of recorded history, was hers to chronicle for good or ill. The weight of her responsibility in this, the final countdown before the most powerful nation in the history of human civilization blasted off into a new era, barely registered.

She had arrived at the studio early to avoid the crush of New Years Eve traffic in the Nation's Capital. Katie passed the time between reviewing her notes and patiently submitting to the attentions of the network's make-up artist. Her investment in regular workouts at the gym had paid off. Despite the rounds of holiday season parties and dinners, she had not gained an ounce of fat. She tilted her head upward and critiqued the image in the mirror. '*Not bad for a thirty-seven year old, not bad at all*' she thought.

The artist was working her cheekbones now with a soft brush, happily chattering on about a very nice man he would be seeing tonight "he's so sweet and thoughtful, and handsome." Alon bent to her ear -"you'd eat your heart out darling." Katie smiled "that's wonderful Alon, I'm sure tonight will be special for you." It would be a special evening for her as well.

Tonight, millions of viewers would be watching her appearance on "NightWire" the highest rated interactive cable/internet news magazine show in the industry. The host of "NightWire," Matt Frank, a media star in his own right, would lead a panel discussion of Katie's New Year's Eve, 2008, editorial column in the Washington Post. Katie knew Matt Frank understood the issues and largely shared her opinions and interpretations of those issues. She would be the only live guest in the studio with Matt. Other commentators to be featured on the show would be piped in from various locales as well as call-ins from the viewing audience. Her columns had been featured before and Katie was comfortable with the format of the show.

She closed her eyes and leaned back in the chair and sipped mineral water through a straw. Alon was good. He saw that she was getting ready for game time and fell silent. Katie reread her column in her mind. It was full of the optimism of the day...

OUR CHILDREN HAVE RIGHTS TOO...
Katie Stoner

Never before in the history of mankind has an era of peace, prosperity and security beckoned with such tangible force. Man has seemingly triumphed over himself. Digital currency and the New Economy are already transforming our lives. We shall enter the New Year as a newborn society, a world society, steering space ship earth toward ever widening vistas and infinite possibilities.

And yet, for some, there are fear and loathing of the changes before us. Fear of some horrifying apocalyptic calamity to befall us as a nation. Perhaps we, as a species, have been somehow programmed to irrationally resist change. War and revolution are often midwives to the birth of progress in human society. Tonight in many homes across America the pain of labor will be intense. Some have already decided they will have no place among us. Some have already vowed to refuse to participate in the new economy thus denying themselves, as well as loved ones, free access to the many benefits now at hand. Some have already left for other shores, or moved to remote back country redoubts, arming themselves with weapons and stockpiling food, portable generators and all manners of survivalist gear. They have chosen to become refugees in their own country.

I have to ask why. Is mere convenience and security evil? Is freedom from criminals who commit fraud and forgery, who rob and steal, pass bad checks, traffic in illegal narcotics, evil? Is progress itself evil? Should we have abandoned the genetic research that ultimately provided a cure for cancer, or the cloning techniques that have allowed us to repair traumatic injuries to the spinal column, freeing the disabled from a life sentence of quadriplegia? Should we regret the eradication of HIV negating the certain death sentence of AIDS? Should these extraordinary medical and technological achievements have been prevented because they were evil? Can there be any evil more deadly than ignorance?

The Renaissance itself was largely a struggle between the forces of religious superstition and the forces of reason. Not only were scientists targeted by the religious orders of the period. They went after their own kind as well. Religious heretics were often tortured to death. On occasion, the victim's bodies were exhumed in order to burn the corpses. The point here is not to equate modern ecclesiastical faith with the excesses of the past, but to question why the unreasoning ignorance of that violent and tragic period continues to echo in this age.

It is universally accepted that one of the greatest evils is the love of money. Note here that money is not evil. Indeed, there is no morality to consider when one considers money. There are however, things one may do with money, or to get money that may be good or evil. It is redundant to say again that the majority of crime, whether we are looking at narcotics trafficking and abuse, or illegal prostitution, gambling, money laundering, burglary, theft, robbery, or the general corruption and greed these offenses breed are all facilitated by money-anonymous paper money.

The street gang members, who peddle poison to our children, terrorize and destroy neighborhoods, and in the end destroy themselves through violence and addiction are just one example of what we seek to eliminate.

Why have we allowed an underclass of despair to flourish in our midst? Crime is a communicable disease. The vector, from the beginning of time, that facilitated its spread, was a worldwide system, a global economy awash in anonymous coinage and printed paper money. We have a vaccine now – it's called digital currency. It has and will forever change our culture. It simply will eliminate profit for criminal activities. The evidence is in and it is compelling. Certainly, we can attempt to turn our backs on progress. We can pretend to not know better. We can join flat earth societies. We can even wistfully pine for the 'good old days'. Should we ever do so, just be prepared to go back to more prisons housing more and more violent offenders in a rotating door criminal justice system. That is the legacy of the good old days.

America has been, and shall always be a nation under God. It has never been and never shall become a theocracy. America is a nation of great goodness, not evil. It is a nation steeped in a tradition of tolerance for religious freedom of expression and freedom of worship. Religious freedom of expression is a basic constitutional right.

Just be sure to remember and to heed as well, our children have rights too – the most basic of which is the right to be properly nourished, clothed, educated and protected from the consequences of irrational decisions made by their parents that they cannot unmake to save themselves.

Matt Frank peeked around the dividers, "Katie, air-time in five minutes, you look marvelous." Katie laughed "Thanks Matt. Better be careful with your compliments though, Alon just might demand a raise."

**

CHAPTER SEVEN

New Years Day, 2009
Soddy Daisy TN

Art and Keith grinned as they watched the big rig pull away from the roadside diner. The driver didn't know he had picked up a hitchhiker. The load of telephone poles he was hauling all the way to California from South Carolina now contained a little electronic tracking device nestled in the voids between the logs. It hadn't taken them long to find and remove it from Keith's car. It had been concealed above the sheet metal bracing of the trunk hood and secured with electrical tape, obviously a rush job. It was Art that found it. Keith had been removing the rocker panels when he heard Art whoop "Got ya!" Keith's contribution was what to do with it. Art had listened to the plan, done a quick morality check with his conscience and finding no conflict there, said "let's take the pickup and find a nice ride for our little buddy."

Art and Betty agreed that Keith was welcome to stay and were delighted to see him recuperating from his week on the road. He had lost the sallow look in his eyes and though he was prone to long periods of silence when it seemed as if his thoughts were a thousand miles away, he had begun to smile again. Keith was feeling better. Art had kept him busy. It wasn't hard to do. There were plenty of projects and chores that Art had meant to get around to completing.

Today he was going to repair the sluice run from his stock pond. As they rode back to the property, Art explained what the problem was. Years ago, he had devised a plan to generate electricity by rigging up an old Sperry Rand electric motor to a water-driven flywheel. The hydro power was provided by tapping into a stream that flowed down from the North face of Signal Mountain. The device worked fine and generated more power than Art used. The local power board figured out pretty quickly that Art's meter was running backwards at the retail rate and set him up with a meter that allowed Art to sell his excess electricity at a wholesale rate. The checks he received each month had helped to pay off the mortgage on the property. The runoff had been diverted to his stock pond, which then required a sluice gate to control the water level. Keith had been amazed. Art just shrugged, "it seemed like a good idea and it really wasn't too hard to do. It keeps me busy clearing the pipes and keeping trash out of the intakes."

Keith looked out at the winter brown fields and clearings rolling by and thought how little he had done to prepare himself. He didn't even have his guns now. None of his good stuff, the SKS assault rifle, the M-16, and his favorite-the 1943 vintage M-1, was registered. *'If they find me, the bastards will hit me with everything they possibly can'.*

They were home again. Art nosed the truck into the driveway and pulled it up to the barn doors. As if reading Keith's thoughts Art jumped down and turned back to Keith, "let me show something you might like," and disappeared into the barn.

Keith, curious to see what it might be, stepped into the opening. Art was gone. The barn was neat and orderly, the light from the doorway filtering in the dusty air.

"Where are you Art?" Way toward the back, a section of floor raised up, and Art's head popped into view, "back here Keith," he called. Keith blinked in surprise 'so Art has a little hideaway huh?' This was totally cool. A staircase led down to a landing and then to the right where it opened to a large chamber. Art pulled a string and a bare bulb illuminated the interior.

"I believe this used to be a moonshine operation years ago. I found some bits of cork and pieces of old copper tube."

Now Art was grinning again "I went to the courthouse and looked through all the old microfiche and drawings of the farm and buildings and there's no record of this anywhere."

Keith looked around the space, the walls appeared to be some kind of masonry work. Home canned jars, neatly labeled and dated, along with freeze-dried food packs, reference books, medical dictionaries and "how-to" manuals populated shelving systems along the walls. The floor was flat mountain stones and concrete. He touched the wall "It stays dry too doesn't it?"

Art nodded, "Like a bone."

Keith followed Art into a series of rooms. A computer work station and digital dish receiver was set up in a nicely furnished space that opened into a larger cavern furnished with odds and ends of old couches and armchairs, garage sale stuff mostly. A locked glass front wall cabinet contained some very useful and interesting gear: a Remington Model 700 with 3x9 power scope, a Ruger 30-06 with scope and tripod, several Colt 1911 model 45 cal. automatics and three shotguns - 12 and 16-gauge and an old 4/10 over - under.

Keith touched the glass, "my Dad had one of these," pointing to the old combination shotgun/22cal piece.

"I know. It's a beauty. We're about twelve feet underground now. You can heat this place with a match. Take a look at this Keith."

Art led the way to the last room. A small kitchen area with a coal stove and a privy behind a set of café doors completed the tour.

"I think we could make it pretty comfortable down here. I ran some extra electrical outlets in a while back..."

Keith cleared his throat "Are you saying I could stay down here Art? Cause if you are, you're probably saving my life."

Art just grinned at him "it ain't the Ritz Keith, but I bet you ain't gonna mind that, for a while anyway."

Keith's eyes teared up "I don't know how I'll ever thank you enough..."

Art walked past his friend and slapped him on the back "Just don't start brewing "shine" on me. Come on Keith, let's go up to the house now and see what Betty might be doing in the kitchen." Keith pulled the light string and wiped the back of his hand across his eyes, "I'm right behind you man."

**

January 1, 2009
Boston, MA

John had argued with Dawn about going into work and was still a little pissed off about it. "It's a holiday Dawn. Hello, anybody home? Jesus."

Dawn had wrinkled her nose at the sight of John stumbling out of the bedroom with his hair in snarls and a big sheet burn across his cheek. "Look, I'll be back before you even get in the shower. You're just going to sit around in your pajamas and watch the games on the tube all day anyway. I won't be long. I promise. I just need to run a few sets and then I'll stop."

John just shook his head and headed for the coffeepot.

Dawn peeked her head back in and called out "I'll be home for lunch," and closed the door.

John turned on the TV. Dawn never learned to like college football. No problem, John hated golf, which was Dawn's favorite sport. "That's why we have so many damn TVs in here." At least she made a fresh pot of coffee before she left. It looked like it was going to be a nice day. January thaw? Too early John decided. He settled in for the pregame show. Michigan was gonna get creamed.

***

CHAPTER EIGHT

New Years Day, 2009
Washington, D.C.
IPTF HQ

'In retrospect' he thought later, *'I should have stayed at home'.*

The phone call just ended provided ample cause to regret not having done so.

Deputy Director James Dodd slowly and carefully replaced his phone in the cradle, the enormity of the caller's terse report swelling in his chest and roiling his insides. *'Jesus Christ. Oh God no. Oh Goddam no, not now, for God's sake, not Dawn!'*

Dodd's chest heaved, gasping for air, sick, sickened, and sickening, his mind searched for an accommodation and found none there. Lamely, *'There must be something wrong with people'.*

He cradled his face in his hands and rocked back and forth, stupid, senseless, moaning-unaware he was doing so, *'There must be something really bad wrong with anyone who could do this to another human being.'*

He didn't want to believe it still, but there it was, Dawn had been shot in the head. Assassinated right in front of the Federal Reserve Bank Building in Boston-at close range, they had identified powder burns in the entrance wounds. Her driver was still alive but in a coma and probably wouldn't live the night. Dawn had died immediately.

Witnesses said they heard two rapid "double pops" in succession and turning to see what the noise was described a tall thin man in a ball cap and long overcoat walking rapidly away from the curb where the limo had been parked. Dodd closed his eyes against the image. *'Broad daylight in downtown Boston and nobody knows shit, saw shit, gives a shit. God Damn it'!*

'How could somebody just walk up to an attractive, decent, caring woman and just execute her in the street?'

"Oh God. John O'dea. He doesn't even know." Dodd picked up the phone and ordered his car brought around. He punched a new line and placed a call to Tim Thurston. No answer. "Christ."

Secretary again, "Tammy, get the Citation ready, and have the pilot file a flight plan to Boston. Get the Director for me and patch him to my car phone. Get me the new girl from communications, and have her meet me in the garage. Try to find Carpenter and get him too, and for Christ's sake let's keep this on ice until I can reach O'dea."

Dodd was moving down the passageway fighting a feeling like water in his guts. At the doorway marked 'gentlemen' he made a dive for relief and lost. *'What a fine day this is turning out to be'* was his last thought before he emptied the contents of his bowels from both ends.

His secretary was good, one of the best. Head down, Dawn's friend, Tammy Davidson, began making the calls, ticking off the tasks she had to complete. No one would have noticed anything amiss. They wouldn't have seen the single teardrop that splashed onto her neat and orderly notes, smearing the purple ink and mottling the smoothness of the paper.

***

January 1, 2008
South Station
Boston, MA

Carl was clean. The gun was in the Bay. He had changed clothes simply by pulling off the old ones revealing the fresh set underneath. His overcoat was reversible and he turned the khaki side inside out hiding the blue side he had been showing when he made the hit. His old clothes and baseball cap were in the battered attaché case that he was carrying in his hand. He would unload these when he arrived at his next destination. His ticket to New York was in his hand and the train was about to begin loading. *'Nice piece of work'* he thought as he idly glanced around the station.

Carl was fastidious in his planning and flawless in his execution. Normally, he preferred his hits to appear to be accidents. This client had insisted that the hit be obvious. "I want people to know this was no accident." No matter, Carl was happy to oblige. "The customer is always right"was his motto. Payment had been confirmed through his bank in Bangkok. $200,000.00 up front and he expected to see an additional $300,000.00 now that the hit was done.

Carl wanted to retire. This hit was his parachute. Things were not going to get any better for Carl in the new economy. Cozumel, Mexico was his destination, departing Kennedy Airport in about five hours. Carl boarded the train.

***

Unknown to the general public, and initially, even to the Boston Police, twenty-four hours a day, seven days a week, tiny digital cameras installed by the IPTF were recording every event at the Federal Reserve Bank Plaza.

It would be several days before this information was shared with the Boston authorities. In the meantime, IPTF special agents were running and rerunning the digital video of the murders. The quality was remarkable. The cameras could read newsprint at 50 meters.

Unfortunately, there was little to be seen of the assassin's face. The bill of the ball cap and dark sunglasses effectively shielded it from the prying eyes of the surveillance systems. He was gone. He had simply vanished without a trace.

There were a lot of very unhappy people and the special agents were taking out their frustration on the video technicians. It looked like he was a white male between the age of thirty and fifty. A blowup revealed one clue for what it was worth, he had worn two sets of clothes, a brown pants cloth edge had appeared momentarily from beneath the subjects right trouser cuff. Mensuration of the imagery revealed that the subject was approximately 6'1"tall, probably 175 lbs., hair color light brown, possibly long stuffed up into the ball cap–not much to go on.

There was one other item. The suspect was wearing a rather large and bulky timepiece on a wide Velcro type wristband. One of the agents remarked that it appeared to be a type of chronograph worn by professional scuba divers. It didn't help that the Boston Police Dept. was loudly blaming the failure to apprehend a suspect on the IPTF for sitting on the videotape for three days.

***

CHAPTER NINE

January 6, 2009
The World Trade Center
New York, NY

The International Law Enforcement Association conference was on break. The attendees were greedily descending on the excellent spread laid out for them—bagels and cream cheese, fresh fruit, granola and gourmet blended coffees.

IPTF Director Tim Thurston had been introduced as the keynote speaker. Tim's carefully scripted and touching remarks regarding the tragic and senseless violence that had taken Dawn Fenstermachers life had hushed the room. Many of the attendees had known John O'dea and Dawn as friends as well as colleagues. It was a moving moment and there were some bowed heads and furtive eye wiping at the end.

Tim thought he had done well. The bodies of Dawn and her driver/bodyguard had been flown to Washington, D.C. where they lay in state at the Capitol rotunda. POTUS and POTUS-elect had both attended the services and voiced their outrage and grief. President-elect J.D. Waites had spoken angrily of the nations loss of a powerful force for progress and decency, and movingly of the personal loss to those who knew and loved Dawn best.

Even better, the next day the Domestic Terrorism Special Powers Act was blasted out of committee and on to the floor of Congress for a vote. It passed on a voice vote, by acclamation no count was necessary. *'It was beautiful.'*

True, they had tinkered with the wording a little, after all they had to feel like they contributed something to the process, and in joint committee they'd parse it further, but the end product was not in jeopardy. Just so long as it gave Tim a free hand.

Besides, the Fourth Amendment to the Constitution of the United States had already been gutted repeatedly by the Supreme Court during the late 1990's. The Special Powers Act was just a little icing on the cake. Essentially, "unreasonable" search and seizure could no longer be defined. Anything the government wanted to see, do, or seize was just fine, thank you. While Thurston watched from the gallery, he recalled the old saw about frogs being so dumb that they wouldn't hop out of a pan of water if you heated it to boiling-so long as the increase in temperature was slow and steady. As Thurston had informed the President the day of the vote, "I'd say that frog's done."

Thurston glanced at his watch. It made him think of Andy Warhol's shopworn "fifteen minutes of fame" comment. *'Dawn and her driver had already had theirs, what a price to pay.'*

He would be flying back to D.C. himself this afternoon. Extraordinary measures would soon be needed for extraordinary times.

Operation Northern Beacon was near completion. When the time came to root out the hard core refuseniks, the militia nuts and their survivalist cousins, Thurston would be ready, willing, and best of all, perfectly legal. He congratulated himself again for having assembled such a stellar staff.

Come July, Northern Beacon would descend like an avalanche. Specially equipped and trained National Guard and DOD Counter-Terrorism Units would cut through the back country camps and hideouts like a hot steak knife through butter.

How fitting and just it was that Dawn's senseless murder at the hands of a callous assassin should be the catalyst. It had sent just the right signal to all concerned. It wasn't healthy to question the IPTF or the new economy. Dawn had begun to offer unsolicited and clearly troubling opinions on matters that shouldn't have concerned her. More than ever Tim needed to ensure absolute loyalty and security.

.

Dawn, in Tim's opinion, had seemed to lose her enthusiasm for the project, and that, Tim had decided, made her both stupid and expendable.

Dawn's worst mistake had been that she had already finished the protocol. There would be other incidents, other tragedies, Tim knew. Some would be real acts of insurrection and protest. The others he would personally arrange, like he did for Dawn Fenstermacher. Tim was busy making omelets. Some people just had to be eggs.

***

Boston, MA
January 9, 2009

The movers had left. The worldly goods of Dawn Fenstermacher, sorted, inventoried, packed and labeled, were on their way to storage pending final resolution of her affairs. Numb, cold, and silent, John O'dea had sat in his chair and staring unseeing while items were brought to him for identification. It couldn't be, and yet it was. Dawn was gone and he would never see her again. His grief bowed him like a tree bent before a gale. Everyone had loved Dawn. He had loved her most of all. He bent his head and sobbed alone in the dark.

***

Minneapolis, MN
January 23, 2009

"Toni" stamped her feet, flapped her arms, and blew warm air into the cuffs of stiff gloves. She had spent the last of her money, her cash money, on two little rocks of crack cocaine last night. Everyone was leaving town. Cash money was scarce.

She had turned a trick two nights ago in the back seat of a minivan littered with stale French fries and kid's toys. The fat slob she had serviced for $20.00 claimed it was all he had. "The deal was for fifty" she had screamed. He had just laughed at her. "What, you wanna try to rob me? Come on. See if I'm lying. Go on, you wanna pull a knife? I got nothin` ."

At least Toni had the satisfaction of leaving something hard to explain when the pig went home. Toni had strong fingernails-she didn't need a knife. She left him bleeding and cursing, four deep grooves painfully swelling his fat jowls.

Toni didn't eat right on the best of days. The last time she could remember eating... she couldn't remember the last time. *'Jesus it was cold'*. She pulled her hand out of her glove and blinked stupidly at the sight of puffy yellow blisters and wondered if her hands were just dirty or if the tips were really black.

'What the hell? I need some cash. I need to get warm.' Everybody was leaving town. The bus terminal was only a couple of miles away. *'All kinds of perverts ride busses. I still look okay.'* She glanced at the reflection in the plate glass storefront beside her. *'Not good, shit, not good at all.'* Her nose and cheeks were red, not a rosy glow, but raw looking. Toni started to cry. The terminal was too far and the air too cold. She couldn't feel her feet.

The Minneapolis Police cruiser followed at a discreet distance. Officer Lundgren and Ericksen had made three pickups this week. Same shit different day. Lundgren hit the blue light and accelerated "Let's pull her in."

Ericksen gave the siren one half-assed yowl as the cruiser drew abreast of Toni. He climbed out of the car, "Ma'am

would you step over to me please? Face the car please.
Put your hands on the vehicle please."

Ericksen felt along her sides and legs patting her down.
'*Disgusting*'. Her body felt like a bundle of sticks under a
blanket. It was only 20 degrees below zero, not too bad
for Minneapolis. '*This one wouldn't be much trouble.*'

"What's your name Ma'am?"

Toni was shaking with cold. The sky was a cruel blue,
frozen like her. High power lines swayed and whistled in
the wind. Everything was white or black except for the
bitter winter blue sky. A crow flew by. Toni opened her
mouth to answer and the car tilted up sideways and she
found herself listening to the engine as if in a cave.

'*It's warmer here,*' she thought and somehow the engine
noise wasn't so loud any more. Toni's eyes rolled up to
the sky again and the sky ran away, a giant blue shutter
rolling it self up into darkness. The sound of Ericksen
shouting for his partner never reached her ears, she was
floating now in the black, the warmth surrounding her
and keeping her so safe, so warm, and she had been so
tired.

The coroner's report listed malnutrition and exposure as
the cause of death. There were no boxes on his form to
check for the new economy.

***

NightWire
February 1, 2009

"Good evening. We thought tonight, we would look at
where we are, where we've been, and where we are going,
on this, the one-month anniversary of the digital economic

revolution, and it's impact on what we are calling the "new economy." I'm Matt Frank, and this is NightWire."

"Joining us tonight is White House correspondent Kelley Graves, NightWire's own medical correspondent Bonnie Whitman, and IPTF Communications Director, Hal Munday. Our panel guests tonight are Syndicated Columnist for the Washington Post, Katie Stoner, and former White House Counsel, Parker Harrison."

"Kelley, let's start with you, the White House has been in the crosshairs this past week regarding the increasing visibility of grass roots opposition to what some are claiming are draconian implementation measures; not the least of which is the handling of what the media has labeled the "POLIREG" resistance problem."

"That's right Matt. The Administration's Spokesman, Josh Linder faced a lot of tough questions today. Political and religious-based opposition, the so-called "POLIREG" community, has been a continuing source of concern for this administration."

<roll videotape> "The "POLIREGS" seem to be sending a rather clear message to the government and that message is 'we aren't going to play'. What is the President going to do to head off a serious confrontation with these people? And, is it true that IPTF, FEMA, the FBI and Treasury Dept. are mobilizing what has been described as goon squads to forcibly begin rounding these people up?"

Josh Linder: "Sam, I think you know the tremendous success we have had in allaying peoples unfounded fears of the new economy. At the risk of repeating myself, paper dollars, bank checks, and credit cards on dollar accounts are still acceptable as legal tender and will continue to be legal tender without restriction until July 1 of this year."

"Two–this administration has not yet determined that a specific response to isolated incidents is appropriate or necessary."

"Three–The work of the IPTF and other federal agencies is focused on technical and information management concerns and will remain so. This is a time of tremendous change. The changes we are experiencing have not been unanticipated or unplanned. Nor was this transfer to a new economy system expected to be seamless."

"Four–As to goon squads, Sam, I think you know better than that. What we should be talking about are the statistics we're seeing on street crime, narcotics trafficking and abuse. All down sharply. I think we should be looking at the continuing savings on Medicare, Medic-Aid, and Welfare, the sum of which since October of just last year is over fifty billion dollars and will save an additional one hundred fifty billion dollars by the end of this year…"

<End tape>

"Matt, there you have it - some problems, perhaps, but nothing serious."

"What's the mood in the White House Kelley?"

"Overall Matt, I'd say pretty rosy. The stock market is continuing to post gains, and with unemployment approaching a record low near 3 percent, there is understandably a huge swell of good feelings in general, and this President seems to be riding a wave of incredible good will."

"Thank you Kelley. Parker, let's go to you now, what is the legal exposure, if you will, if some of these admittedly bizarre rumors of alleged official misconduct by Federal agencies turn out to have some basis in fact? How will these agencies really expect to deal with citizens that apparently won't enroll in the new economy?"

"Matt, the White House has expressed a strong concern for public safety during a period where, regrettably, tensions in some quarters are running high. The issue here is clearly public safety and the welfare of every citizen. As you know, there have been some attacks by various groups espousing political and/or religious convictions that prevent their immediate participation in the new economy. I am confident many of these concerns will be allayed over time."

"Are they ever going to join our 'reindeer games'?" Matt smiled, in appreciation of his own witticism.

Parker chuckled "I rather think they will Matt. Money as a printed, government issued legal tender was itself a controversial and politically divisive issue as far back as the Presidency of Abraham Lincoln. We didn't even have a functioning Central Banking System until near the end of the Great Depression. Over time, the attitudes of the American people will evolve. I think history will repeat itself with a growing acceptance and understanding of the new economy and all the benefits of enrolling. In time, people will find it difficult to imagine money that isn't digital. We are in the 21st century, and there is no rolling back the calendar at this point."

Matt nodded to the oversized screen in the studio.
"Since we have the honor of the presence of Hal Munday, official spokesperson for the Infrastructure Protection Task Force, let's ask you Hal, are there concerns about

compliance and implementation measures, etc.?"
Hal laughed good-naturedly, "At this point I think you could justifiably say our greatest concern is getting enough rest and trying to deal sanely with an insane work load."

"Seriously Matt, the dedication of the folks at the IPTF is humbling. Many of the people I work with and see on a daily basis, from the Director on down to the most junior enforcement officer or administrative support staff have been working basically around the clock to keep this incredible initiative on course."

Matt pressed again, "But what of the reports of illegal retention of American citizens, and roundups of what have been described as the not so law-abiding denizens of the urban sections of our cities and towns?"

"I think the statistics we are seeing and reading about in the press tell the story best. After just thirty days, the drop in criminal and other illicit activities; fraud, bad check writing, check kiting, tax avoidance, as well as the disruption of a huge underground economy engaged in all manners of illicit activities; narcotics trafficking, gambling, prostitution - I could go on but I won't - is already saving the American taxpayer billions of dollars."

"The days of the "Career Criminal" are over Matt. I firmly believe this is great news for all Americans."

Matt turned back to the camera, "This may be great news for America, but there may also be a downside to this, Bonnie?"

Bonnie Whitman was well prepared. "Yes Matt, despite every effort to contain any possible downside, because the new economy, as expected, is fundamentally so heavily reliant on full participation and implementation, there have been tragedies."

"When you look at the structure of implementation, the legislation and regulations are a grab bag of Federal, State, and even Local regulatory incentives and disincentives that were cobbled together over a period spanning the past seven or eight years. Like all carrot and stick approaches to policy and compliance, there are, unfortunately, gaps that some people are falling through."

Matt furrowed his brows and leaned into his next question. "What, specifically Bonnie, what are the most significant areas of concern to the medical community?"

"Well it's quite simple. There are many children who have not been immunized, who are not being seen for medical problems, nutritional problems, in some cases, we are seeing serious infections and injuries going untreated because parents are not enrolled. When the situation is pressed with the parents, by say a school nurse or administrator, too often the parents are simply pulling their children out of school. Who know what the effects of this may be in terms of stunted social development? Are we creating potentially serious long term emotional problems or disorders as a result? It is just heartbreaking Matt."

Katie Stoner saw her opening and waded in, "This is just the sort of neglect that I have warned the American public about for literally months now. It is not an issue of political or religious freedom. It's about neglect, pure and simple. This administration is going to have to make some progress on this or there is going to be hell to pay and I mean soon." Matt smiled into the camera, "We'll be taking your calls on this and more. Stay with us on "Night Wire.""

***

CHAPTER TEN

February 14, 2009
Cozumel, MX

A moray eel, obviously an old timer, his head as big as a football, gaped silently at the interloper. His home was at the base of a coral head mushrooming from the floor of the Gulf of Mexico, sixty maybe seventy feet tall. There were many coral heads here. Like apartment buildings or huge commercial office towers, the coral heads loomed magnificently, ancient, silent structures teeming with life far beneath the ocean surface.

Carl regarded the moray in silence, breathing easily, slowly, conserving his supply of air. He would need to begin his ascent soon. He checked his dive computer and pressure gauge. Over a half-hour of this dive had been spent at a depth of a hundred twenty feet. His body was saturated with nitrogen. To avoid the bends a strict protocol must be followed. Carl let the current take him, drifting southwest at two knots. The moray remained on station, mouth agape unconcerned with his departure. Carl had time - it was pushing it - but a beautiful valley opened below him. Schools of fish danced in unison, darting as if one super intelligence directed their motion. Carl checked his gauge. He was at 130 feet. Nearly weightless, never the less he descended gently, drifting with the current. A resting nurse shark noted the alien presence and with a lazy flick of her tail disappeared into the haze.

'Soon', Carl reminded himself. He was an experienced diver, he knew the limits and could compute the ascent in his head. He knew his easy deep breathing pattern stretched the limits of the one-hour's worth of air in his tank.

The colors at this depth were not as vivid. Carl didn't care, he was alone and that suited him fine, fifty-two minutes on his chronograph. Most divers would have begun the ascent ten minutes ago. 'This was the best' he said to himself. A feeling of great joy swept over him - no people, just Carl and the deep blue sea. He felt he could fly like a bird beneath the surface of the shimmering sea - depth gauge, one hundred fifty.

Elated, Carl executed several rolls like an aerobatic barnstormer, small, intensely purple fish with black dots swam with him. Carl looked again at his watch, checked his pressure gauge and dive computer. 'No shit, you're pushing it Carl. . . . .'

Carl didn't care. Carl didn't know he had been given a special tank filled just for him. The pretty, newly hired young clerk at the dive shop had seen to it that Carl was provided with a potent cocktail mixture of various gases to include nitrous oxide. Carl was getting seriously shit-faced at 170 feet below the surface. Carl's last bit of reason informed him that the tank must now be nearly empty. He was now sucking to get a lung full. At this depth, without sufficient pressure in the tank he would be unable to draw any air at all. Carl regrettably began his ascent. At 120 feet, much to his alarm, the air was gone. Exhaling slowly he continued to rise. At eighty feet he managed to suck one last half lung full of air. He waited for a count of thirty and began to ascend again. His head was a little clearer now, clear enough to know he was ascending too fast. There were no good choices, he could drown or get the bends - neither option was attractive to him.

At thirty feet the first symptom hit. His joints began to throb and his eyes seemed to want to pop out of his head. Panicking, he burst the surface and ripped off his mask and regulator as the full impact of the bends hit him.Waves of excruciating pain were exploding in his head and joints. Carl screamed in agony. A scream heard only briefly, his wail extinguished by the sea as he rolled into a ball and the waves covered his face.

What remained of his sanity briefly flickered with the suspicion he had been given a doctored tank. The new girl at the dive shop had insisted in loading the heavy tanks herself. "Happy Valentines Day" she had said. 'The bitch.' Carl ground his teeth so hard his upper right incisor snapped off. His body locked in a rigid vise, Carl knew he was finished, knew he would die unable to even control his own limbs. His weight belt assured a gentle descent into the abyss. Carl opened his mouth and breathed deep of the sea. He thought of his money sitting in a bank in Bangkok and wondered what they would do with it. *'What a strange thought–what a strange thing to think. . . .'*

Carl blacked out, his body twisted and contorted, slowly relaxed in death. Beyond the shimmering membrane above him, sea gulls circled and swooped. The sun glittered on the sea.

***

February 15, 2009
HIDTA HQ,
Boston, MA

"Fair Winds and Following Seas," proclaimed the homemade banner now drooping sadly from the ceiling. John had cleared out his desk the day of the reading of Dawn's will and settlement of the estate. Now a week later, his colleagues had thrown him a little party.

'Good people', John thought. He would miss them. Both "gag" gifts and real ones were in a plastic bag by his feet. John stared out at the bay. He didn't need to work anymore. Dawn had seen to that. Even after leaving a large trust fund for the care of her parents, John had been amazed to find there was still close to eleven million dollars that Dawn had bequeathed to him.

His secretary, Joan, had stopped by and wished him well. She had to 'beat feet', she smiled, "the kids were probably destroying the house." She had meant to give him a buss on the cheek and at the last moment, feeling his loneliness she had given him a hug and a kiss instead.

People were making 'it's time to go' noises and some had already left. John had no one to go home to and the inertia of that knowledge held him in his chair. Still. . .

there were things he thought of doing. The investigation into Dawn's murder was going nowhere. John had not been hopeful that it would. John knew a professional hit when he saw one. The revelation that the entire plaza was under video surveillance, a fact that even the Boston P.D. had not known, interested him.

The video, shown on TV over and over in the days following the murder revealed one fact to John. The murderer had known the cameras were there. The killer would never be found, he was sure of that, but whoever had ordered the hit could not be so sure. John was not going to just fade away. Whoever had hired this murder would be hiring again. John would be watching and waiting. He had time. He had lots of money.

***

February 23, 2009
Renaissance Center
Southwest Region
Gallup, NM

The transports were arriving daily. Southwest Region was filling up. Alan was exhilarated. He and the others were working long shifts but there was a sense of excitement in the air. Sure, a lot of people were looking pretty messed up when they first got here, but it was amazing just how quickly they seemed to calm down. Sometimes the really nutty ones had to be physically separated from the rest and placed in special dorms.

It bothered Alan to see that happen when it meant separating family members. *'But shit man, if they just behaved a little better and even tried to act reasonable, that wouldn't ever happen.'* Alan just figured some folks were too high strung to get with the program - at least for a while.

Alan was doing good though. Because he seemed to get on well with people he had been made a "greeter." Kids seemed to like him. That helped him to get the parents to cooperate. Not like there was any good reason why they wouldn't. *'Hell a lot of 'em were just tired and scared and usually hungry.'*

Alan found that it was best to get the new arrivals fed right away. The food here was even better than what they served in Muscle Shoals. He figured it was just having a full belly that calmed 'em down a little. That was certainly, partly true, but there was another element Alan wasn't aware of. Every plate in the commissary used to feed the new arrivals was washed, sterilized, and then rinsed in a special solution. The solution would evaporate leaving a tasteless, odorless, dried residue on the plate. Chemically, the residue was similar to the date rape drugs of the late 1990's. In carefully measured and controlled quantities, the drug was exceptionally effective in relieving anxiety and stress. All Alan knew was that he was more likely to get a wan smile or a grudging handshake from the new arrivals after they had been given a proper feed.

Sometimes Alan would help to escort people to appointments at the medical center. Some people were pretty worn out and that meant they were susceptible to disease. The Center's first priority was to immediately identify and treat any illness or injuries. They had taught Alan all this stuff so that he could help explain things to people. It was sort of like being a tour guide Alan thought.

Alan stepped up to the door of the bus. First rate transportation. The buses were air-conditioned with deep cushioned benches for maximum comfort. There were built in child seats for the little ones and extra pillows and blankets in the overhead storage compartments. You couldn't see who was aboard though because the windows were so deeply tinted. They were averaging three or four buses a day, seven days a week. If the bus was full, Alan could expect to greet sixty-five to seventy passengers. He would only work one bus every four days though. Four days on–three days off, with a new group every week.

There had been a few scuffles but that was really rare. Alan had never had any trouble. They taught him that too. People tend to follow the herd when you put them in a group. Get the first one to cooperate and they all fall into line. Besides, by the time they got to Renaissance Center Southwest, they were pretty resigned to the situation.

The bus door opened with a swish and a U.S. Marshall stepped onto the pavement. Alan accepted the zip disk listing of the passengers. The Marshall was going off shift, and he wasn't in the mood for small talk.

"Single file please, we don't want to lose anyone." The first passenger descending the steps looked to be about nineteen years old, wearing a silk windbreaker and bright neon high top sneakers. Alan smiled and nodded to him and pointed to a painted line on the pavement.

"Welcome to Renaissance Center. If you would, help us get organized and form a line here. We'll be going to the Commissary for dinner in just a few minutes." Alan was doing a good job. He helped the children and the older people off the bus. He could have been a politician working a rope line–same deal really.

***

Dr. Clarence Darby, Renaissance Center Southwest, pressed the clip of his pen activating a hidden sub-aural frequency beam generator. Clarence was a clinical psychologist. Well, he was going to be one someday. He was just an intern at the moment.

The person he was interviewing, Mr. Patrick C. Eire was having difficulty appreciating the benefits of the new economy. Although Clarence and he had made great progress in connecting on a personal level, Clarence felt he had made less progress in persuading Patrick that he was misguided in his refusal to be registered.

Clarence was reading aloud from his notes the description of what Mr. Eire had endured in the days and weeks preceding his arrival to the Center. The desperate days rummaging in trash containers searching for food and perilous nights spent shivering with cold, wrapped in layers of cast off blankets and old cardboard, hiding in the shadows beneath the overhang of a Freeway ramp on Interstate 80. Clarence reminded Mr. Eire how it was then living in fear, the uncertainty, and the terrible loneliness he had felt.

As he did so, the low frequency audio waves Mr. Eire was being bombarded with would increase in amplitude and power until Clarence clicked his pen again. It was a very subtle thing. Research on non-lethal weapon technologies had shown that feelings of anxiety and nausea could be induced in individuals or even large groups by beaming sub-aural tones at just the right frequency. Applications for this technology had been projected to encompass everything from non-lethal dispersing of domestic political demonstrators to protection of United States Embassies from rioting protestors. It was soon discovered that it worked quite effectively in clinical settings as well.

Whenever Clarence wanted to induce dread and anxiety in Patrick he could. Conversely, when he spoke of the new economy and the very fine work being done at the Renaissance Center to help people see their way clear to become a part of the new economy, Clarence would click off the pen.

When Clarence felt that he had made some headway in persuading his subject of the right path and had gained some agreement, a very fine atomizer nozzle in the table would begin to administer small doses of a mildly euphoric aerosol. Good cop/bad cop refined to a new level.

Mr. Eire felt the nausea returning. Clarence was obviously a good kid. He had certainly treated Patrick with every courtesy and respect. Now, just the memory of being on the 'outside looking in' was making him feel sick, *'and for what - because some folks would die rather than accept the mark of the beast? These are decent people here. I feel like I'm the freak. Hell, I have kids that are Clarence's age. He's a nice kid. He's just trying to help'.*

Aloud Patrick said, "look, maybe I have gotten this all wrong, you people have been awfully good to me...."

Clarence smiled, "I hope we can work everything out. We're just trying to help folks get used to some changes that seem hard to accept. We understand. Believe me; we really do." Clarence clicked his pen and hit the aerosol switch with his knee.

Patrick felt a peace stealing over him, like the grace of God descending. His anxiety seemed to vanish.

"You know Clarence, I believe you do understand. I really do."

Clarence patted Patrick's arm, "let's talk again after dinner. I think everything is going to be okay."

"I think so too, I don't know why, but I really think I may be waking up from a bad dream. Thanks for talking to me Clarence. You know, I have a son your age…"

***

CHAPTER ELEVEN

March 1, 2009
Boston, MA

David passed his hand under the scanner. Taco chips and salsa, a six-pack of Sam Adam's Ale, a Boston Herald newspaper, total $12.39. The rowing team was doing well. His thesis, writing itself practically, and the prospect of an overdue break in the weather and springtime in New England should have buoyed his spirits. Yet, they weren't. David knew why.

John O'dea was still in mourning. Every time David looked into John O'dea's eyes, he saw the grief and the rage, and each time he felt he was somehow responsible. It was as if his father's beliefs were to blame, and that he, as his father's son, was indicted as well.

David loved and respected his father, but, and this was a big but, some asshole - grief for his father swept over him. With the same bullshit ideas as his father, had heartlessly blown away a woman he had grown to admire and respect. 'Loved even,' David thought as he stuffed his purchase into his knapsack.

David had not gone home. He didn't want to face his father thinking the thoughts he was thinking. Every thing, every freakin' thing was upside down. The economy was blazing, people were working, buying homes, investing, public schools were finally reversing decades of declining scores, and other than infrequent reports of banal incidents of domestic violence, drunken brawls in bars and similar relatively innocuous events, the streets were safer than they had ever been. Any normal person would be celebrating the arrival of the Kingdom of God on earth, and yet they weren't. People like his dad were having none of it.

David started his car and waited for the windshield to clear. "Cold and damp with intermittent showers, highs in the low thirties," the perky voice proclaimed from his dashboard. *The world was full of good news. Bad shit never happened to you or anyone you knew.*

David scanned the newspaper. Today, a reporter in the Herald had described a new experimental Federal Corrections Facility in Reno, Nevada. It was called "The Retreat." Built to receive and process both federal and state penal system convicts, it was apparently implementing what David thought could only be described as mercy killing. The article had dealt rather differently with the topic. The article had explained that the success of the Regional Renaissance Centers in facilitating re-entry to society for both nonviolent criminal offenders and "POLIREGS" had spawned not one, but two new initiatives.

The other initiative, "RIDS" for Restructuring Initiative Developmental Sites, was even more impressive. We were emptying the prisons and for once, the inflow was less than the outflow. David remembered a statistic from a criminal justice class he had as an undergraduate. Thirty percent of the prison population in America was serving time for bad check writing. *'Come July, there won't be much chance of that,'* he thought.

The article was well done. It was full of the current "aren't we so freakin' smart to have figured it all out and finally doing something about it" bullshit that most stories seemed to reflect. In fact, as he read on, despite his better judgement David thought it did sound pretty damn reasonable.

According to the article, RIDS provided rehabilitation screening, treatment and "outcome selection" for convicted felons. There were three options for prisoners processed through a RIDS facility. The first and statistically most prevalent was eventual reassignment to a Renaissance Center. The second was continued treatment at the RIDS facility. The last was reassignment to The Retreat. The Retreat housed inmates with no possibility of parole. The gist of the article was if you seriously screwed up at a RIDS facility there was only one destination, "The Retreat."

In the article the reporter profiled a "Retreat" inmate who had petitioned the State to "MOS out." To "MOS out," was prisoner slang. It was an acronym for "Modification of Sentencing." "MOS" was an option for all the inmates of the Retreat. It was a purely voluntary program. "MOS" was executed only through a notarized and "fully informed and explicit consent" by the inmate petitioning for modification of sentence.

In this instance, the petitioner was a thirty-five year old white male. At the age of twenty-eight, Tommy Ray Anston had murdered his wife and three young children. After first drugging his wife, he had suffocated his sleeping children in their beds and then set the house on fire to hide his deeds.

Tommy Ray Anston had been arrested, tried and convicted, sentenced to death, which later on appeal, was commuted to life without possibility of parole. He had already been incarcerated for five years prior to his transfer to The Retreat. For a man Tommy's age, life without parole represented a span of fifty or even sixty years in a 4' x 8' cell.

Tommy Ray wanted out. Before "The Retreat," for people sentenced to life without a possibility of parole, suicide was the only escape. Now there was another option. You could elect to modify your sentence. A decision to "MOS out" was not really suicide. Legally, and this was important, it was technically an elective, state sanctioned procedure available to all inmates serving life sentences "without a possibility of parole."

Tommy Ray had a mother. He was not close to her. She, in turn, was horrified by what this child of hers had done. Tommy Ray had never known his own father. Mom was old and ill. Close or not, she was the only and last person on earth who had any thought for Tommy Ray at all. What the hell, she could at least get the money.

Inmates who requested a MOS were given certain dispensations and rewards. For those, like Tommy Ray, who were concerned with the well being of a family member--it had to be a blood relative--opting to MOS provided for a $250,000.00 lump sum payment to a named beneficiary - more money than Tommy Ray would earn in prison if he lived to the next millennium.

An attorney, appointed by the federal government at no cost, would represent Tommy Ray and execute the required documents. Tommy Ray would have to complete a mandatory two-week waiting period in which to change his mind. At the end of the two-week waiting period, again with legal representation, the requesting inmate would sign the final authorization for clinical procedures to effect sentence modification.

MOS was a one-time option. Once initiated, you could renege. You could live, but you could never again request a MOS. There was no appeal. Tommy Ray had not blinked at eternity. He had signed the documents and the machinery was set in motion. Like a game show host, the bailiff had read into the record what Tommy had won.

"Pursuant to the request for modification of sentencing in the case of Tommy Ray Antson, same order is hereby granted and entered into the record. Seven days from today clinical procedures to effect sentence modification will be administered as requested and agreed to by both parties. A lump sum payment of $250,000.00 is assigned to named beneficiary Lily Jean Antson, biological mother of Tommy Ray Antson."

"Tommy Ray Antson by order of this proceeding, is to be immediately transferred to the interim receiving facility for further preparation for sentence modification."

"While in the interim receiving facility, conjugal visit privileges, private apartment housing and special dietary allowances to include requested meal menus, alcoholic beverages and authorized medications are approved and mandated. Spiritual counsel and visitation is authorized and encouraged."

"Appropriate entertainment facilities to include sports activities as agreed to in this proceeding, as well as video and audio selections as provided for within the aforementioned request for modification of sentencing package are hereby granted."

"The People wish you Godspeed and commend your selfless decision for the benefit of your survivors and assigns. You are hereby released to the custody of the interim receiving facility transportation deputy."

'Who wants to live forever anyway?' David turned his attentions to finding an opening in the traffic. He hoped John would be glad to see him. Maybe the Sam Adams would help. David didn't have much else to offer.
***

Chapter Twelve

March 15, 2009
Restructuring Initiative
Developmental Site (RIDS)
Moline, IL

The Tri-Cities, Moline/Rock Island, IL, and Davenport, IA, had grown modestly over time into a conglomeration of cities, suburbs and villages that while centered in the continental mass of the United States had no center of its own. The "heartland" of the heartland was essentially soulless. Indeed, one would question the very existence of this triad of grubby, soiled and tired urban sprawl. Why here, and then, why at all?

A regional mental health facility in Moline had been recently converted by the ubiquitous IPTF into a model demonstration of enlightened criminal justice processes in the new economy. As always, progress was at hand. The denizens of this, the newly proclaimed first of many Regional RIDS, were not, as a rule, particularly law abiding Americans. At the same time, they were not, by careful review and screening, violent offenders.

Like Alan, many Americans were imprisoned for offenses of less consequence than what most would consider dangerously aberrant behavior. Drug addicts, abusers of illicit drugs, check kiters and bad check writers, Deadbeat Dads, and white-collar criminals had overpopulated the prisons of the United States long before the new economy.

Again, like Alan, these were the unlucky, the careless and the overreachers who had pushed the envelope of a tolerant and forgiving society. In the past, they would serve their time, get early release for good time served and, until their luck ran out, return to the comfort zone of petty criminal enterprise, placing the burden of their failed lives onto the overworked and justifiably cynical parole officers in whose care they had been placed.

There was little question as to whether they would return. Recidivism was the norm. The absurdity of the situation was sublime. Each return to the harsh embrace of the "System" imparted new criminal knowledge and increased cynicism of the criminal justice system.

Jerry Carpenter had determined there must be a better way. His views had expanded over the years and captured a growing constituency within the halls of power. It was Jerry who really foresaw the new economy and it's many implications. It was the advancing digital information technologies and the potential for sweeping change that had given birth to the new economy.

RIDS was an initiative that encapsulated Jerry's thoughts on the question of why there must be crime, murder and violence in human society. Renaissance Centers were like halfway houses. RIDS was the real effort. It was in the RIDS program that Jerry saw the eventual restructuring of traditional ideas and policies regarding the resolution of a panoply of criminal and aberrant behaviors. There were two areas Jerry felt were beyond present methods of intervention: sexual predation and cold-blooded murder. Manslaughter and crimes of passion were not excluded from the criteria for selective assignment to a RIDS facility. There was certainly a wide field of endeavor for one committed to a belief in a cure.

The first reality to convey to the occupants of the RIDS was that the world had changed. There were options available to them, but the options available were not the ones they had access to in the past.

Crime was, after all, a retail endeavor. It demanded an anonymous store of readily available and universally acceptable unit of exchange-cash money. Muggers, robbers and thieves occupied the lowest rung of the criminal hierarchy. Cash money constituted the coin of the realm. More sophisticated thieves could work in forgery of checks and financial instruments. Further up the scale were the experts in credit card related theft and fraud. The highest echelon was the hackers and hi-tech thieves who entered into banking and financial fraud.

The low-level illicit drug traffickers and users were also in reach. To succeed each required an anonymous exchange of value. Now that cash had been eliminated, the opportunity to return to old habits had been eliminated.

The huge dilemma now was "what does a thief do?" RIDS intended to resolve the dilemma once and for all.

To Jerry Carpenter it was a structural issue. The new economy provided the structure. The occupants of correctional facilities nationwide would have to be restructured to adapt. Recidivism was no longer an assured outcome. The opportunities were removed. and yet, these people had to engage in some means of support. Jerry saw each life as a point on a moral plane. The plane was a continuum of cause and effect, which in one direction constituted the future, the other the past. To either side was good and evil. The future direction lay in the consequences of the choices one made. Development of a strategy to provide a framework of choice for people who often felt no choice existed was necessary.

The enabler, the facilitator, the compass of all prior choice had been the old economy. The RIDS program had a new economy. Jerry would give them each a new compass. Now the future had a new paradigm. In the past were the prisons of the old economy. The current point in the plane was the Restructuring Initiative Developmental Sites. In the future lay the Renaissance Centers and eventual re-entry to society. For some, the future would lead to "The Retreat." One thing was for sure. There would no longer be stasis. By one path or another, Jerry would lead and tend his flock. God and Mammon. One did not choose. They were the same. Jerry would free them all. Crime was retail.

***

March 21, 2009
Soddy Daisy, Tennessee

The ground shook beneath him. Closer in, the blast waves were snapping trees off at the base like twigs--rolling

Thunder on the Ho Chi Minh Trail, Cambodia. At this distance the sudden change in air pressure produced only a slight nausea.

High above the river valley, massive B-52 formations were sowing their seed with callous indifference for the inferno they were creating below. No one, man or creature, caught in the primary target zone would survive. Art's team had called in the strike passing the coordinates of the NVA units in the valley below.

Suddenly the footprint turned. Horrified, Art watched as the explosions began to march up the ridge toward their position. It was like a nightmare! Art tried to move but everything was happening in slow motion.

Art turned toward his radio talker, Staff Sergeant John O 'dea scream ing, 'No! Target zone is zero niner zero! Stop! Stop! Friendlies in the Fire Zone!'

John looked up from the radio handset and smiled. The advancing explosions were drowning all sound.

Art tried to reach out to take the handset but his limbs would not obey. John winked at him still smiling. He covered the mouthpiece with his hand and mouthed silently, 'Dawn says Hi. I'll tell her you called.'

Art screamed in pain as his eardrums burst. John suddenly left the ground and seemed to hover in the air above him, his silhouette black against the firestorm arching into the sky. Now both John and Art were flying, tumbling through hot orange light, light bright as the sun. Art screamed as the crushing force and blinding heat seared him, forcing the air from his lungs 'NOOOOOOOOOOO!'

Art's eyes snapped open as he gulped for air. Betty gripped his hands. "Art. Wake up. You're okay Honey."

He sat upright, body rigid, his eyes wild and unseeing. Betty soothed him. "It's okay. You're home. Just a bad dream, you're okay now." Outside the first real thunderstorm of the season was crashing. The panes rattled in the wind. Art slumped a little as the room came into focus. He exhaled shakily.

Art looked around the bedroom in the gray chill of twilight. Twilight had been his time to operate, it was his friend, the dark was his trusted companion, his unit patch had proclaimed:

82nd
AIRBORNE
LRRP
"WE OWN THE NIGHT"

A phantom smell of cordite tinged with the mildew stench of decaying jungle undergrowth was still in his nostrils. Betty gently released his hands. A bead of sweat trickled down the small of his back. Betty spoke to him low and gentle, she had seen this before, but it had been years since the last one.

"It's almost morning sweetheart. Why don't we get up and make some coffee? We can sit by the window and listen to the rain."

"I dreamt about John."

"I know."

"I think Dawn was in it too. Not in the dream, but John was talking to her. I don't know." Art scrubbed his hand through his graying hair. '*It was all pretty crazy.*'

Betty put on a housecoat and pulled back her hair. "Maybe what happened to Dawn and now having Keith here and everything else..."

Art pulled on a pair of David's old sweats. "Maybe. I haven't dreamt about it for a long time." They walked down the stairs to the old country kitchen. Art and Betty had left the old pump handle and washbasin in place. Betty moved the handle up and down three times before pure spring fed well water gushed out of the spout. Art stoked the wood stove. It still got chilly at night. The rain was falling steady now and the wind had died down.

Betty set the battered tin percolator on the stove and sat down across from her husband. She reached out and took his hands.

"I've been thinking about Keith. He's feeling a lot better now and maybe it's time he made some decisions."

Art nodded. "The Lord brought him to us. I don't know what the Lord has in mind for Keith. Keith knows we're praying for him. He might not yet understand that God loves him. The only thing Keith can do to make things right is to trust Him and give his life to Him."

Betty looked down at her husband's hands. She was afraid. Verses from the Word filled her mind with dread. '*Lest those days be cut short there should no flesh be left alive.*' She shivered in her housecoat.

'*Virtue, hard work, loving obedience and piety had not*

delivered Job from his test before God. Who am I next to a saint like Job?'

She squeezed her husband's hands.

"Take this cup from Me," God's only Son had prayed to no avail. It was the will of the Father. In the end, Jesus had cried out in the agony of death, "My God, My God, why hast thou forsaken me?"

Betty's hands shook.

Art gently raised Betty's face to his. "We are His and He will not forsake His chosen."

Betty nodded, tears rimming her eyes. "I know." *'I just can't help being afraid.'*

Art pulled her close and held her in his arms. She rested her head on his shoulder and closed her eyes. *'Please God, don't ever take him away from me.'*

The old-fashioned percolator gave its first bubbling pop. The rain continued to fall. Art rocked his wife gently. The smell of coffee brewing filled the room.

***

CHAPTER THIRTEEN

April 3, 2009
The White House
Washington, D.C.

President Waites idly examined the cuticles of his carefully manicured nails. The signal he was sending was both clear and deliberate, *'get to the point soon or risk losing my interest entirely.'*

The Attorney General of the United States, the Honorable Lawrence Carson Killebrew III, reddened slightly with embarrassment.   Lawrence was not insensitive to the cues of his President. "I was simply suggesting Mr. President that the IPTF may be overreaching on the timetable."

The President turned to Tim Thurston, "Well Tim, you are the Director of the IPTF, it seems Larry has some concerns here."

Tim Thurston relished the chance to swat this Ivy League prick but now was not the time. Still, he was pretty sure he could get this pompous ass to make a fool out of himself in front of his old friend J.D. Waites, the President of the United States.

" Mr. President, the Attorney General, as always, has my deepest respect and admiration. I am sorry to say I believe his concerns, demonstrate a regrettable lack of current information, for which I take full responsibility."

Thurston looked down humbly for a moment and shook his head as if to say, *'I've been working so hard to make this all come together...'* "The press of business has been enormous and we are all understaffed in the short term. As you know sir, the IPTF has, through tremendous personal sacrifice by all hands and an unparalleled commitment to achieving mission objectives, moved this, the new economy, forward with breath taking speed. I am sure the rapid evolution of RENAISSANCE has left more than a few departments and agencies gasping for breath."

Tim smiled understandingly at the now completely red-faced and furious Attorney General.

"Mr. President!" Lawrence jumped to his feet. He didn't look well.

"Justice has not been left gasping for breath, and if I lack current information it's because too goddam many people over at IPTF think they can play 'I've got a secret'."

Thurston studied the ornate ceiling of the oval office. *'You are so predictable Larry. It's almost not fun...'* Lawrence was on a roll now.

"The "Director" of the IPTF might try to remember who

his friends are. Last time I checked Tim, Justice can open any investigations into any federal agency at any time I find it appropriate to do so."

The Attorney General sat back down and glowered at Tim.

The President chuckled, "Now this is a lively discussion. Perhaps we could all benefit from a short recess. Tim, could you give us just a moment here?"

"Yes sir, I'll see if I can get Sally to rustle up some refreshments for us. Lawrence, can I get anything for you?"

The Attorney General, suddenly realizing how easily he had been had, mumbled "No thank you."

"Mr. President?"

"Sure Tim, see if Sally can set up a tray for us. I'll be just a minute. I'll buzz Sally, OK? Thanks Tim."

Thurston closed the door to the oval office and accosted Sally, the Presidents Personal Secretary.

"Sally, the boss would like a tray sent in. He'll buzz you when he's ready - the usual, some tea, ham sandwiches, you know what he likes. I'm gonna take a little stroll myself. Stretch the legs. Thanks Hon."

Sally smiled "Sure thing Director."

Tim walked off with a satisfied smirk. *'What a useless shit. How the hell did a total loser like that ever rise to the position of Attorney General?'*

In the Oval Office the President had wheeled around in

his chair turning his back to his Attorney General.
"Springtime's coming Larry." It was true. The grass was
greening up and the hedges were sprouting bright new
shoots.

Killebrew waited, "Yes it is Mr. President."

"I really do love the change of seasons. Change is what
we're about here. I need to know if we're all on the same
page with that."

Waites spun back around in his chair. "Tell me something
Larry, we've known each other for quite some time now,
longer than either of us care to count."

The AG cleared his throat, "Yes sir, a long time."
He shifted in seat wondering 'Where the hell is this going?'

"Yes a long time. I need to know if you're with me on
this Larry."

"I know I got a little excited Mr. President. Tim tends to
push my buttons. He acts like he thinks he's a goddam
Cabinet Secretary. I'm not alone in that regard. He's
pissed most of us off repeatedly for the last four years."

J.D. Waites smiled and looked down at the desk blotter
with the Seal of the President of the United States. 'It was
never easy. It was the hardest job he ever had really.'
"Larry, I kept you on because I needed continuity at the
Justice Department. All of you gave me your resignations.
I didn't accept many of them."

The President now looked Lawrence directly in the face
eye to eye. "I felt we really had enough to deal with
without breaking in a whole new team."

'Christ! This SOB is firing me!' Lawrence's face began to redden anew. " I'm afraid I don't understand..."he began. "I think you do Larry. The seasons are changing my old friend and as hard as it is to accept, it's time I made some changes too."

"Because of that snotty little shit," Lawrence roared, "I'm shown the door and that smug little bastard stays? You have my resignation sir. When do I leave?" Lawrence stood, hands trembling with rage.

"Sit down Larry. Stop making an ass of yourself. I have a folder for you to review before you leave. I think we should not engage in unproductive displays here." The President waited for his words to sink in. Then, more gently, "Larry, sit, please."

The Attorney General accepted the folder and sat down. There were photographs, statements, credit card billings, bank accounts, liaisons and encounters his family would never understand. He closed his eyes. *'You evil bastard.'* "I understand Mr. President. You have my full support as always."

The President beamed "I like you Larry, and I think you're doing a hell of a job. I wouldn't think of losing you. I just needed to make some changes. We weren't working in harmony sometimes and I think it's important we all understand how the team works and who the coach is."

The President buzzed Sally, "Sally? Roll that tray in will you?"

To Larry, "Have lunch with me. I'll get Tim to join us. What do you think?"

"I'd be delighted Mr. President, of course. Thank you."

Lawrence's heart was palpitating badly and he was struggling to keep his emotions in check.

"Great! Just super! Sally? Have someone run down the Director and have him join us for a quick bite. Thank you."

"You're very welcome Mr. President. Oh, they have the pumpernickel rye that you like..."

"You're my girl."

Sally giggled and checked the tray one more time. *'What a nice man the President was. Just a Prince'*, she thought.

***

April 7, 2009
Deer Antler, OK

"Folks around here don't need no "federal guvmint" to tell us how to get by. Seems to me them fellas in Washington kinda got the wrong idea 'bout who runs things here, and it sure as heck ain't them. This is Oklahoma and we're doin' jus' fine thank you."

Earl Angsley rocked back on the homemade porch glider and looked out over the rolling hill country.

"Been here since this was the Injun Territory, my daddy and his daddy and his daddy before him. This here's 'God's Country'. Pert' near 2,000 acres and I own every inch. I pay my taxes and I take care of my own."

Freelance correspondent Judy Klein was doing a piece for the Oklahoma Star. *'Earl was the real McCoy.'* Judy was enjoying the visit immensely. *'This sure as hell isn't New York City.'*

Judy sipped her iced tea and jotted notes as they talked.

"You just mentioned taxes, Mr. Angsley. Now as I understand it, you and your family, in fact most of your neighbors haven't enrolled in the new economy. Come July, how do you and your neighbors plan on paying your taxes on your land?"

"Miss Judy, you seem like a nice enough gal. Now fancy talk about enrolling in the 'new economy' as you city folks call it don't wash round here. We're proud people, proud to be what we are. It ain't fancy and citified round here but that don't mean we're ignorant."

Earl stopped to light a smoke, expertly cupping the match against the fresh spring breeze that was swirling the detritus of winter fall oak leaves about their feet.

"My daddy always told me you don't call a man down off his porch unless you're ready to give it a go. Now that's plain talk for you to put in that paper of yours. We got cash money and we'll pay our taxes just like always. If the guvmint don't want to accept that then I guess me and the guvmint are gonna be fixin' to go round and round."

"Are you suggesting that you'll fight if the tax collector has to take your property for unpaid taxes?"

"Miss Judy, I ain't suggestin nothin'. This is my land and I intend to stay on it. I intend to send in my taxes in cash money and I 'spect the guvmint will accept my payment."

"And if the government declares your payment is unacceptable?"

"Then I guess it's the guvmint's problem. I ain't gonna worry about it. I can grow my own food, raise my own pork and beef and chicken. I got a trout creek right on my land and more deer to hunt than I could ever need. I don't need no computer money and I don't need no help. If need be, I know how to defend my constitutional rights too. My daddy taught me and I taught mine. Family, God and Country. I 'spect most folks round here believe the same."

"Mr. Angsley, many Americans are wondering what defending your constitutional rights really means. I think most people view that kind of talk as a threat against the duly constituted government of the United States of America. Are you really saying that you and your neighbors would fight against the Federal Government? Would you fire on American Law Enforcement Officers or if it came to that, declare war on the government?"

"Now listen up here Miss Judy. I know you're jus' doin' your job asking all these silly questions and I don't hold that against you. I really don't. I think you're a fine young lady and I can tell you been raised right. I served my time in the military and I did my duty. I didn't need no body to tell me what my duty was. If anyone declares war on anyone, it won't be us. The guvmint might declare war on us I don't know. Like I said, it ain't too smart to call a man down off his porch less'n you're fixin' to give it a go. If it come down to that we'll be ready."

Judy found herself nodding in agreement. "I believe you will be, Mr. Angsley."

"Why don't you stay for supper? Hannah's set a plate for you already hopin' you'd like to stay a spell."

Judy looked at her watch. If she hit the road now, she could be back in Oklahoma City by dinnertime. She checked her notes again and looked out over the expanse of prairie, winter brown and bristling dried blackened twigs, the tones of winter broken now by patches of green and clumps of early spring blossoms. The grip of winter giving way to the earths slow tilt toward the sun. She admired the stately island of oak trees, thick and gnarled, planted for windbreak and shade years ago, by whom? *'Earl's great Grandfather?'*

A city girl and a thoroughly modern one at that, she wondered at her own sense of peace and contentment sitting here on a simple country porch, Earl's home built glider squeaking in its tiny orbit. These were good people she decided, and she feared for them.

She thought of her own childhood, parents divorced, she and her sister raising themselves while their mother pursued her own career and "identity." To her great surprise, she found herself wanting to cry and moved by her emotions, she stood up and before Earl could stop her, gave him a quick kiss and a hug. She managed to choke out a thank you for his hospitality and wished him "God Speed" and wondered again as she did so what the hell that meant.

She fled down the gravel drive to her BMW and jumped in. The late afternoon sunshine was gilding the low hills of the Oklahoma prairie. Butter yellow light seemed to infuse the very air. She really was crying now, and she really didn't know why.

***

CHAPTER FOURTEEN

April 15, 2009
China Town
New York City

Hsiao Li scanned the terrified occupants of the van for a familiar or at least friendly face. He and his family had paid their life's savings to the "Snakeheads" to bring them to America, to New York, the "Emerald City." The Snakeheads were well paid.

His wife and daughter had missed work today. They were too sick to work. Racking coughs and frighteningly high fevers. Hsiao had purchased herbs and prayed for their recovery. He feared a beating from the boss. He was used to such occurrences, but he feared deportation even more. Slowly he and his family were paying off the Snakehead who had smuggled them to the States. He had hoped to be free of the monster by summer's end.

Hsiao Li groaned in terror. *'What to do?'* He had been working at his sewing table when the warning bell had sounded. Curses and shouting had filled the air and everyone was running about looking for wives and children. Hsiao Lee's wife and daughter were sick and alone. He must not be separated from them. He would hide!

He had crawled into a bin of fabric scraps and waited trembling as the sounds of wailing and pleading slowly subsided. Carefully he had waited for a full half-hour. He raised his head and peeked out. The shop was empty. The banks of fluorescent lights were off. Very little light penetrated the incredibly filthy windowpanes. Hsiao dropped to the floor and crawled between the rows of commercial sewing machines. Like a dog, he scurried beneath a cutting table for cover and peered down the dank graffiti-festooned stairwell. It was the service stairs. He would sneak out the back and try to get to his tenement. He prayed silently for his family and bolted from his hiding place.

Eight floors down he flew. Fear and panic surged through his thin body. *'What if they were gone? What if the agents had come to their building first?'* Terror gripped him and he groaned again. His cheap sneakers worn through in the toes slapped on the stairs echoing dangerously. Finally, he reached the bottom and burst through the ancient six-panel wood door. To his horror he ploughed right into New York City Policeman, Officer Zeke Badowski. Hsiao screamed in terror as Officer Badowski regained his balance and calmly brought his nightstick down on Hsiao's head.

"Looks like you missed one Danny."

Immigration and Naturalization Service Special Agent Danny Ellis laughed, "They are a sneaky lot Zeke. Ya didn't kill the little guy did ya?"

"Nah. He'll be okay. Little shit could run couldn't he? Wonder if the NFL will ever have one for a tight end?"

"Ha ha ha, yeah right, he could play in the 'rice" bowl."

"Yaaa, gedadda heah. Hey, hey, Danny, how bout the 'fish head and rice' bowl huh?"

"Yeah yeah yeah, okay, load em' up huh Zeke? They got that accident cleared and I wanna get this load outa here."

Hsiao was stunned but not unconscious. It didn't matter. He spoke little English anyway. Zeke lifted the little man by his shirt collar and half-walked, half-dragged him to the back of the van.

The van door slammed shut and the bolt snicked into place. It was over. He would probably not find his family again. There were rumors of camps. He looked around him for any hope and found only despair. Hsiao drew his bony legs up and rocked back and forth, tears streaming down his thin face. 'The Emerald City.' Hsiao wept.

***

April 19, 2009
Cross Walks Grill
Madison, WI

The long deceased, yet eternally adolescent Kurt Cobain
was keening a grating, atonal dirge over the club's sound
system. It was just past ten in the evening. Business was
brisk at Cross Walks-Madison's premiere party bar for an
aging generation X crowd. The club bouncers were
watchful for over indulged guests. Rule one was, keep
the Cross Walk's tables productive. If you were going to
continue to occupy limited precious space you had better
be buying, the line forming outside the club waiting to
get in demanded no less.

Bobby Ogelsby, age thirty-three, white male 5' 11", 170
lbs., light brown hair, blue eyes, sat at the bar. Bobby had
made a fair amount of money in the cocaine trade before
the new economy had put the squeeze on his clientele.
They had been well to do professionals for the most part.
Bobby dealt in quarter ounces typically, occasionally more
if a big weekend was planned. He was well connected
and could, if the customer so desired, deliver any quantity
of high quality blow.

The Dominicans and Haitians had displaced the Mexican
drug trafficking organizations that had once controlled
the midwestern distribution of cocaine. They had needed
guys like Bobby to tap the high-end market. Bobby was a
'stand-up' guy. He moved a lot of product and that kept
both his suppliers and his customers happy. More
important, thanks to his rather elite customer base, Bobby
could count on a phone call from friends in City Hall if
anything was about to go down.

Bobby was not a criminal per se. He tended to view
himself as a clear-eyed opportunist. His last transaction
for cocaine had been in mid-February. Bobby had cash

reserves set aside in anticipation of the new economy. He was down to about thirty thousand dollars now. Lately he had been considering leaving Madison. Wisconsin winters sucked.

Bobby set his glass down. A glance from Bobby was all Eric, Cross Walk's hardest working bartender, required. Scotch whiskey, single malt, neat and no delay. Eric was eager to please. The single malt Bobby preferred was stocked just for him. Bobby was the best tipper in the bar and he always paid in cash.

In Bobby's realm, allowance was seldom made for fools, but as long as a fool's words or deeds did not intrude upon or otherwise offend Bobby's personal space or sensibilities, Bobby preferred to live and let live.

Unfortunately, tonight, offense would be given. The offender was Sammy Parris, Cross Walk's Head Bouncer and general pain in the ass. Bobby had always had a special hard-on for overbearing, loud and abrasive individuals, but to his credit, Bobby understood and allowed for the reality that assholes like Sammy Parris were fairly numerous and would always be so. His own inclination to deal harshly with the Sammys of the world was an impulse he could certainly control so long as people like Sammy had sufficient good sense to avoid a direct challenge.

Bobby gazed, bemused at his old childhood friend at a nearby table. Passed out cold and far from caring, Denny Sweeney, harmless drunk and local ne'er do well, was face down at his table in a small puddle of saliva snoring contentedly, oblivious to the opening blast of Hootie and the Blowfish as well as Sammy's vigorous attempts to rouse him.

"Hey Shit Head!" Sammy roared, "Hey! Wake up!" Bobby watched the scene unfold dispassionately. It looked like Denny was not going to give Sammy boy any satisfaction. Bobby snorted and sipped his single malt, *'Ol' Denny was shit-faced and that was a fact'*. Sammy, asshole emeritus, attired in his faggy-ass body builder muscle shirt, was clearly getting frustrated.

Bobby watched as Sammy grabbed and shook the unconscious man by the back of his collar. Denny's head flopped around like a puppet. One eye opened briefly, perused Sammy, then he grinned good-naturedly and managed to slur out "fuck off asshole" and promptly passed out again. One of the occupants of a nearby table laughed.

What happened next wasn't as funny. Sammy, muscles bulging heroically now, spun Denny around, lifted him off the floor and propelled him head first into the wall. Like a human crash test dummy, Denny crumpled, slid to the sticky carpet and lay motionless.

"Get up you piece of shit or I'll kick your freakin' head in!" The laughter trailed off. At the bar, Bobby's hands tightened involuntarily. Once, twice, three times, Sammy kicked Denny half lifting the drunk off the floor with each impact. On the third kick Bobby snapped.

Bobby cleared the distance, almost 10 feet from his barstool to Sammy, airborne, his cocked left elbow smashed into the bouncer's temple. Sammy staggered sideways, dazed by the blow. In a fluid motion Bobby grasped two hands full of Sammy's greasy blond hair and yanked down and forward into the path of Bobby's catapulting right knee. Blood from Sammy's nose and mouth sprayed like a fountain. The explosive impact snapped Sammy's head up and back. The body builder's thick neck, exposed and defenseless, invited destruction. In a blur of motion,

Bobby snapped a massive ridge hand into the target. Sammy's trachea collapsed with a flat splatting sound.

Sammy lurched backwards, strangling, eyes bulging in pain and terror. Panicked and choking Sammy clawed at his throat. Had there been a doctor in the house, or even a paramedic, to attempt an emergency tracheotomy, Sammy might have survived. Slipping into shock, he began to lose consciousness and dropped to his knees. He looked up at Bobby as if seeing him for the first time and fell sideways onto the floor. A pathetic gurgling noise, an odd whistling bubbling sound, was his last testimony.

Bobby didn't wait. He threw a fifty on the bar for Eric and picked Denny's rag doll ass up off the floor and hoisted him across his shoulder. No one offered to get in his way. 'It was inevitable' he thought. Bobby had always known, someday, somewhere, some stupid shit thing would happen and he would lose his temper and someone would end up dead. Denny groaned a little as he laid him out on the back seat of his car. People were pouring into the parking lot and running to their cars. The good citizens of Madison Wisconsin weren't about to hang around and wait for the cops to arrive.

It had happened so fast–in less than three seconds–Sammy kicking the shit out of Denny and then Bobby standing over Sammy watching him die. There was blood everywhere and some chick had started screaming "oh my God he killed him." Bobby looked at his reflection in the rear-view mirror. He wasn't even breathing hard.

Bobby pulled out of the parking lot and headed south toward old County HWY. 61. Where he was headed, he had no clue. Denny wasn't likely to contribute to the plan.

Bobby turned on the radio. "Fly like an Eagle" was playing.

'Who was that, Steve Miller?'

A gas station was coming up on the right. He would park in the shadows near the bathrooms and get himself cleaned up. Denny too if he could rouse him long enough to hose him down. Most of his 30,000 in cash was safely concealed in a magnetically switched hidden compartment in the trunk. Fortunately, he had just picked up his dry cleaning. He would have to get rid of the car, a late model Mercedes Benz sedan. Bobby looked at his Rolex watch. He could be in St. Louis by morning.

***

April 20, 2009
St. Louis MO

Former Police Officer Chris Rose surveyed the empty apartment. EZ Storage had accepted her cash payment for a six-month rental. The Department had not accepted her membership in the Missouri Minutemen. She could have quit the Minutemen, enrolled in the new economy through the Police Departments Human Resources Department and accepted a one year probation and kept her badge. The offer was genuine and her colleagues had urged her to accept the terms.

This afternoon Chris would drive to Chattanooga. She had worked hard cleaning the apartment. To her relief she had not found any electronic devices. At least the Feds weren't interested in her. She was pretty sure she would get her deposit back. She could use the cash. Like many young women she spent about what she made and had little in savings. Her pension plan had been worth almost $17,000.00. She had been able to get it in cash

after a long hassle and filling out a bunch of forms designed to discourage and harass anyone demanding cash vice a digital transfer. It would have to do.

Chris was anxious to see Keith Randall and hoped yet again that he was anxious to see her too. Chris walked into the empty bedroom. *'Dummy! Almost forgot the phone.'* Miraculously, just as she had bent to pull the plug on her bedroom phone it rang.

"Hey 'Cool Breeze.' I'm looking for a lunch date. You free or do I need to take a number?"

'Bobby!' "Bobby Ogelsby, is it really you? Oh God you don't need to take a number. I'm buying. Where are you?"

"Well, I'm not really sure Chris, in a phone booth; I know that much. Looks like Hawthorne Ave., 1200 block."

"Don't move. I'm just finishing my walk through. I'm moving. Oh my God Bobby, if you had called two seconds later I'd have never known you were in town. Stay put, I know right where you are. I'll be there in fifteen minutes okay?"

"No problem Chris. I'll be here. Ciao."

Chris looked at the phone in her hand for a moment before reaching down and pulling the plug from the wall. *'Bobby Ogelsby, what a shock. . . .'*

Chris looked up. The leasing consultant emerged from the bathroom and smiled reassuringly.

"Everything looks just great Chris. We're sorry to lose tenants like you. If you'll come to the office we can scan a transfer of your security deposit. You'll be getting a full refund of course."

"That might be a problem Joan. I'm not enrolled. Can you just cut a check?"

Joan hesitated, and cleared her throat. "Well you see Chris we could have at one time, but "Elmwood Corporate" went digital effective January 1. We can still accept cash and cash instruments. We just don't have the ability to remit in cash."

"Well, how do I get the security deposit back?"

"The deposit will be there for you Chris, don't worry about that. As soon as you're enrolled, we can transfer the funds to you. Until then, it is retained in escrow and no one can touch it. It's completely secure."

"I understand. There is no other way then?"

"I'm sorry Chris. We have seen this over and over. The quickest fix is to get enrolled right away. I would have thought that working for the city you would be enrolled automatically."

"I was 'grand-fathered.' Anyone hired by the city after 2005 was enrolled as a condition of employment. Most of us enrolled anyway, but they couldn't require it if you were hired before 2005, at least until last week. I left the Force because they said I had to enroll to keep my job."

"I see." Joan's demeanor was markedly cooler now. '*What did these idiots expect?*' "Gosh look at the time. I have a showing in five minutes. I really need to get back to my desk."

Joan strode to the door. She paused for a moment a little ashamed of her unspoken opinion. *'No need to pile on more when someone was already down.'*
"Good luck Chris. It's been a pleasure having you with us. Just pull the door shut when you leave, okay Sweetie? Bye now."

"Sure Joan. I'll see you later." *'Fat chance'* Chris stopped at the door and looked back at the sterile living room. *'Empty room, empty life, empty future. Shit, I'm depressing myself.'* She closed the door. *'Bobby, what a great guy.'* Bobby was the last person she had expected to hear from.

***

Chapter Fifteen

April 30, 2009
Soddy Daisy, TN

Denny's ribs were taped up pretty good. Chris had done the best she could to make him comfortable. Sober for over a week and mending, Denny was looking better every day. '*What a strange crew*' he thought. Keith was a cool old dude. Art too, and Betty was the nicest lady he had ever met. True, he wasn't too sure about how he fit in, but no one seemed to look down on him.

It had been a rough few days for Denny. Sammy had done a job on him. Bobby had almost certainly saved his life.

Denny listened as the others talked. Denny had always felt apart from people in general. Hell, he was a drunk-not so much of a drunk that he couldn't hold down a job, but a drunk none the less.

Bobby and Keith were not arguing but it was apparent that Chris was a source of tension between them. Chris was trying her best to be loyal to both. When sleeping arrangements were made, it was clear that Chris would share Keith's bed. It was equally clear that Bobby had other ideas. Their hosts, Art and Betty Chandler were dealing with their own issues.

Events were moving fast. Denny and Chris could still opt to enroll in the new economy without consequence. Keith and Bobby were, as far as they knew, fugitives whether or not they enrolled. Art and Betty viewed life through their own prism. God ruled the universe and they were His subjects. Nothing beyond that reality could shake them.

Denny had not enrolled in the new economy because he didn't feel like enrolling. It was like any other detail or chore he typically avoided. He was a plasterer by trade, and sober or drunk, he was good at his work. He preferred cash at the end of the day and contractors could always be found who were willing to oblige.

Denny had lost his driving privileges years ago. As far as he knew, he was the least likely to be on any body's database other than his regrettable driving record.

Home for Denny had been a furnished studio apartment near a fire station in the urban center of Madison. His refrigerator was stocked with beer and little else. He typically ate once a day when he was working. When he was not, he usually ordered in a pizza. Denny's life had been simple. He worked to earn money to drink. He drank until his money was gone.

Denny rubbed the taping on his ribs. Whatever else he could expect he knew that things were getting ugly in America. He knew that this strange crew was part of an endangered species. That was how it worked. Natural selection. Evolve or perish. There was food here, and shelter. Sober for the first time in many years, Denny was afraid. 'Where could he go from here? What would happen to him? What would happen to them all?'

Keith was talking now. "We need to do something more than just wait for the government to gather everyone up. We need to turn ourselves in, hope for the best, or get busy fighting these bastards. There's no place to run to and no place to hide."

Bobby was shaking his head. "Look Keith, all this shit is gonna happen no matter what people like Art and Betty have to say about it. I had a cash business. My customers disappeared. In two months whatever cash I have won't buy shit. The only thing I can do is enroll and turn it in. If we stay here, nice as it is to have a place to stay, we're going to be swept up like everyone else."

"That's the point isn't it?" Chris looked up from doodling on a pad of paper. "Art and Betty are great people. I can't stand the thought of either of them trying to beat the system. They will lose. Look. I'm a cop okay? At least I used to be. You can't fight this and win. We need to get the hell out of Dodge. We have some cash. We can get out. We can take Art and Betty with us. This place is a trap. You don't think they'll do a Waco here?"

Keith shook his head, "I've talked about this with Art and Betty. They are going to 'trust God'. They say they have prepared for the worst and they are going to stay right here and wait for whatever happens. They're not afraid. They won't fight. They won't leave. They will help as many people as they can. They helped me and they're helping all of us."

Bobby spoke, "Keith, wasn't Art some kind of Special Forces guy?"

"Yeah he was. I've gone hunting with him. The guy's scary. He moves through the woods like a ghost. I've never seen anything like it."

Chris asked, "What about leaving the States? Why don't we just get a sailboat or something and get the hell out? We could go down to South America, Central America, Costa Rica, or Panama. We could ride this shit out and see what happens."

Keith rubbed his temples. Chris stared at the table. Denny said "Hey Bobby, did you know I used to sail boats when I was a kid?"

"Yeah, my old man had a '34 Hunter, kept it at a marina in Chicago. I took classes. Coast Guard Auxiliary, Naval Cadets, I did all that shit, used to win a few races. I can sail a boat. No problem man."

Bobby, "How much does a sailboat cost Denny?"

"Depends, we could get a forty-three or forty-five foot sailboat used, might need some work. It would sleep five or six easy, seven in a pinch. Fifty grand more or less I would guess. We could get out of the country. We would need money for food and fuel. Money for maintenance -

shit, lots of money for maintenance-sailboats are money pits."

Bobby,"Keith? What do you think?"

"I'm broke man. Hell I was broke before I split."
"Chris?"

"I've got some cash, about sixteen grand."

Bobby,"I've got twenty-eight thousand.
Keith stood up and stretched."You all can get a sailboat if you like. I'm sticking it out here. When the time comes, I think Art just might be willing to fight."

Bobby sneered,"Yeah that's great Keith. Who you gonna fight? The grocery clerk? Where you wanna start? We're screwed, and that's it."

'I'm splittin.' A lot of people are heading north to Quebec. I don't need this shit...'

Chris felt hopeless. Bobby was dear to her. He was an old friend and a friend in trouble. She didn't want to lose Bobby. She smiled sadly. 'I've known some really bad-assed cops, but Bobby's a force of nature. He's good-hearted, but man he could be cold - cold and deadly. Why couldn't they stick it out together?'

'Keith and Art were close. Keith would do anything for Art and Art for him. Bobby looked out for Bobby. Maybe it was best if he left'.

Still, she hoped he would stay.
***

May 1, 2009
The Free Idaho Republic Militia (FIRM)
Hayden Lake, Idaho

LTCOL Harry Brandon studied his maps. *'Time to shit or get off the pot.'* When Major Harry Brandon retired from the Corps 8 years earlier, he looked forward to a quiet life with his young wife and family.

Harry had joined the Corps at seventeen to escape a hard scrabble life in South Tacoma Washington. He had applied himself and risen through the ranks earning a degree and commission along the way.

He had mustered out in 2000 having spent the last eighteen months in the Kosovo Republic of Yugoslavia. The Serbs never did give an inch. Although they had been forced into partisan warfare and no longer held any part of Kosovo by day, the bloody bastards sure as hell owned it at night. Harry never got a scratch but of the 800 men in his Battalion Landing Team, only 200 would make it home.

Sick of death and carnage and the frustration of fighting an opponent that always eluded his grasp, Harry had returned to his family and opened a small hardware shop in Boise Idaho. Harry's Hardware and Notions rarely generated more than a few hundred dollars over expenses each month.

Fortunately they had Harry's retirement and his wife Lillian worked part-time at the bank down the street. The first year had been pretty happy. Unfortunately, Harry had time on his hands and a computer connection to the internet to fill it.

He contributed e-mail and news articles regularly to conservative web sites like "The Last Republic" and "Truth in Media."

The gap between the government and what it was in fact up to, and the government as portrayed in the mass media, began to widen until it was apparent to Harry, that the national media and the government were really one. He had been outraged when his wife had actually brought home a how-to manual on a new Federal Reserve "Voluntary Program" called innocuously, "Know Your Customer."

She had tried to calm him down.

"Look Harry, they already know everything about everybody somewhere in all the records and lists that are kept. Look at what the military has on you after twenty-six years of having security clearances and background investigations and the like. It's no big deal."

"That may be" Harry had said. "But I was in sensitive jobs. I could understand the need to check up on me. What the hell is the government doing peeping in everybody else's window?"

She had just laughed. "You worry too much. Besides what do you want me to do, quit?"

Harry had said no. But that night he had immediately scanned the entire document and posted it all over the net.

Harry was pissed but he kept his anger under control for the rest of the year until the next outrage in January 2001--the new National Identification Cards riding piggyback on State of Idaho issued Drivers Licenses.

Again, Harry was off on a crusade. He was becoming a fairly well known presence on the net. His marriage suffered, but it was in 2004 that matters finally came to a head. It was around this time that his business, his marriage and his faith actually began to fail.

First he had been audited and despite being right, he had spent all his savings in proving his point. All the time spent defending himself from the IRS began to affect his business.

He failed to remember to place special orders for his customers, failed to keep track of stocking items in the store, and most damaging, the store was often closed when it should have been open.

In 2004 the new national identification numbering system went into effect. The new number consisted of the old social security number combined with additional alphanumerics to classify the individual by race age gender and religious faith. It also served to track the date of each individual entry into the new system.

That was the last straw for Harry. He went down to the Social Security Administration and tore his card up. Shouting and other unpleasantness ensued and Harry found himself riding home in the back of a police cruiser.

By the next year, Lillian and the children were gone.

"It's the children," his wife had finally screamed. "You're angry all the time Harry. I can't do it. You go and save the world. I just want to save my family."

"So do I." he had roared back.

"Don't you see it's hopeless?" she wailed.

He hadn't answered. He had been afraid to. If he had, he might have relented and begged her to stay. He couldn't afford that. The pain of losing them, Lillian, Jacob and Rebeccah, gnawed his insides. He had to be strong.

The Colonel sighed. He wondered where they might have ended up. *Arizona? Baton Rouge?*

He flipped open the brigade quartermaster report. They were well armed and had, in the manner of the Serb Partisans, prepositioned supplies; food, water, munitions, and basic medicines were safely cached throughout the area of operations.

He was ready. His men were ready too. They were just waiting for the word to go. The longer they hung out here, working regular jobs and caring for their families, the more exposed they became. Still, more people were arriving. How could they deal with the newcomers if they were already deployed in the back country?

True, every new recruit they gained added to their strength. On the other hand, things were moving so fast his counterintelligence people were warning him that they were almost certainly being infiltrated and no one was being properly screened or checked.

LTCOL Brandon, Brigade Commander of the Free Idaho Republic Militia, closed his eyes briefly, *'please God, just a little longer.'*

By July they would be ready. June if they pushed it.

He turned back to his maps. He heard his children's voices, *'I love you Daddy.'* " I love you too" he muttered.

***

May 3, 2009
South Station
Boston, MA

John O'dea was just returning from the Cape. The AMTRACK carriage with its streaky delaminating windows and stiff torn vinyl seats had not made the return to Boston a pleasant journey. Truth to tell, John was sick of the city and looked forward to closing down the flat and leaving Boston for good.

He had spent the day looking the old Cape house over and making a list of little things to repair. He hoped that he might find some peace and comfort in the home where he had raised his children. The flat above the sailing museum was his to do with as he pleased but he knew the place would always remind him of Dawn. The isolation and serenity of the Cape property were what he needed now.

As the little commuter train vibrated and shuddered to a halt, a familiar acrid stench – the smell of hot steel brakes filled the car. John and the other passengers stood and stretched, shuffling with bags and briefcases toward the exit.

As John stepped onto the platform, a large middle-aged man magically appeared beside him smiling broadly.

"Don't make a scene O'dea. We'll be in contact. Don't be stupid."

The man never looked at John. A small package was thrust into John's hand. Without a word, as suddenly as he had appeared, the man disappeared into the throng of workday commuters departing Boston's South Station.

'*What the hell?*' John had been half-asleep when the train arrived. He was fully awake now. John scanned the sea of faces around him-no one seemed to be interested in him or anything else in particular. '*The good ones you can't spot anyway, dumbass.*'

John rarely lost his cool. He had disciplined himself to be so. If you're scared or pissed off, you can't think. Right now, he was both. John slipped the package into his overcoat and tried to think.

The human tide of debarking MBTA/AMTRACK customers was sweeping John along the platform to the terminal. If he ducked left, he could bypass the main terminal and get out via the side open-air entrance. He could at least get some distance between himself and anyone that liked to work close-in with a knife or gun.

John sidestepped a young couple and squeezed past a frantic mother trying to maintain contact with her children and broke free of the crowd. He stopped to light a cigarette-Dawn had made him quit-and looked around again. Everything looked normal, but he had a sense of being monitored just the same. '*Two blocks and I'm home*'. John shrugged up the strap of his overnight luggage back onto his shoulder and left the station. No one followed.

***

Department of Justice
Washington, D.C.

The Attorney General of the United States was not used to being kept waiting. At least he was satisfied that the Director of the FBI had played no role in compiling a folder of embarrassing and politically devastating information on him.   He had hoped and believed that shit had finally ended with the departure of the Clinton Administration.   Cleaning up the cesspool that the Department of Justice had become had supposedly been accomplished long ago.   *'Then along comes the Infrastructure Protection Task Force, the IPTF and its "Director," that fucking little Nazi, Tim Thurston.'*

Well, there were things Larry Killebrew knew too.   *'If everything went right today…'*   His private secure line handset chirped twice.   The Attorney General paused to relish the call and hit the button, "Well?"

"Done deal sir." Lawrence smiled and hung up.

The Attorney General leaned back in his custom ordered soft glove leather recliner.   From what his operatives had told him, it appeared that O'dea was a good man.   Not the best, but damn good.   Soon we'll see how good he is.   The poor bastard just might get lucky.   Then again, he might get dead.   Either way, Thurston and his precious IPTF, courtesy of the Attorney General of the United States, just got handed one more problem.

Although it was likely, even probable, that John O'dea would be very quietly and efficiently removed as a potential problem for the IPTF, the chance that he could connect the dots and solve the riddle was essentially a no risk, win/win gambit for Larry Killebrew.   *'It was shaping up to be a nice Spring day.'*

***

May 4, 2009
Stinky's Pub
Boston, MA

Detective Alan "Skip" Keller, Boston Police Department, Homicide, didn't like what he was hearing from his old friend John O'dea.   Number one, he didn't appreciate that confidential information connected to an ongoing, if badly stalled investigation might have somehow been leaked. Number two, he wondered who was leaking and whether given the circumstances, he had cause to worry for his own safety.

John was looking pretty grim himself.

"Skip, just don't even try to run that crap by me, we've known each other too long. You show me yours, and I'll show you mine."

"Show me what John? Some freak slips you an envelope and now you're hot on the trail? You don't know shit."

"Maybe, maybe not." John leaned forward ticking off the points on his fingers as he spoke.

"I can tell you what I've known since it happened. First of all that bastard that pulled the trigger knew way too much. All those surveillance cameras in the Federal Plaza and not one gets a clear face shot? How likely is that?"

"Two, Dawn and her driver were in the window for this guy less than ten seconds, that's *less than ten seconds* Skip, and the shooter's in position-perfect timing. You think he got lucky?"

"Three, he takes a head shot - double pops each target - textbook black ops, and I'm supposed to think it was some lunatic that didn't like what Dawn did for a living, or that some domestic group of good ol' boys from some shithole militia could put that kind of operation together?"

John leaned back into his chair.

"Come on Skip. Show me what you have. Maybe we can help each other."

Skip sipped his beer. *'Yeah same things bothered me - had a name too and that got yanked at the speed of light. Wonder if John knew that?'*

"I could lose my shield John. Do you know what you're asking?"

"I'm going after this Skip whether you play or not."

"Yeah and I'll run your broken Irish ass in and charge you with obstruction. This ain't Federal John. Besides, you're retired. That makes you nobody. You're a civilian John."

John laughed. "No Skip, you won't. You want to catch this guy as bad as I do. Let's just agree that we never discussed it. If I get jammed up, you can get all righteous and haul me off to jail."

Skip looked hard at John.

'Right-let's get our stories straight like anyone's gonna believe that.'

"I'm gonna regret this John. I swear to God if you get in my way or buddy fuck me even once, you'll regret it worse."

John smiled. '*Things could get worse?*'

"I got a name Skip, Carl James Ennis, former 'Company' man, Operations Directorate - been on his own for at least five years - he's freelancing now."
Skip stared at John. '*That was no freak at the station. This was definitely not what he wanted to hear.*'

Skip hunched forward, his voice low. "Okay, look John, we ran all the departures and bounced everything we had, hookers, snitches, we scooped up everything we could get. We ran every freakin' name on every list, planes, trains and automobiles, everything, Toronto to New York. We got about a hundred hits, small shit mostly, but I had one, one name that popped a match on Interpol. Got it off an airline list, flight from New York to some place in Mexico, Cozumel or something. Guy's been in the shadows on several incidents-all involving assassinations right? So I'm thinking, got ya, ya bastard."

"What name? Did you have a name Skip?"

"Yeah John, this guy uses a bunch of names, all variations on what you got. Carl James, Charley Ennis, Jimmy Ennis, you get the picture. I sent off a request to Interpol for case reports, points of contact, anything I could get, pinged the State Department for passports."

Skip stopped and drank the rest of his beer.

"Yeah, so what did you get?" '*Get to the point!*'

Skip slammed the glass down on the table hard.
"I'm getting to that John. Shut up and listen."

Skip looked around nervously, "This would have been about the next day or the day after, I'm not sure. It's been awhile since this shit happened and I wasn't too happy about it."

Skip took a deep breath. "Okay, so this 'suit' shows up right? And says he needs to see the files on the case. He's got the boss with him. The Captain just says 'show him what you got Skip'."

"So I hand him the case right?"

John nodded. '*Oh God, the bastards went after one of their own, but why?*'

"Christ, I need a beer. You want one John?" Skip signaled the waiter across the bar.

"Yeah sure."

"So this prick in the suit runs through the file right in front of me and pulls everything on this Ennis guy whoever and says 'this never happened. There must have been an error. Understand?"

"So I go, who the hell is this guy? You know Captain McLinn. He's a stand-up guy, he just says 'we understand, no problem'."

"I couldn't believe what I was hearing John. Jesus, if anyone hates the Feds, especially snotty-assed suits like this guy... "

Skips voice trailed off. Skip looked at John sheepishly. '*The boss always liked you John–shit what a fucking thing to say....*'

John waited.

Skip cleared his throat. "Anyway, where was I? Oh yeah right. The boss gives me this creepy look and says 'there's no problem, right Skip?'"

The beer arrived and the talking stopped. Skip looked miserable. John was doing a slow burn himself. *'James Dodd had been the one to call the day Dawn was murdered. But James and Dawn were tight. Besides he wasn't capable. No way James could have been involved. Who then, why?'*

John looked up from the table. Skip seemed really agitated. "What the hell was I supposed to do? Some Fed in a suit shows up and shuts down an investigation, takes my only lead in a double murder and now some joker at the station gives you the same name I was running…"

"Tell me Skip. Did this 'suit' have a name? Did you see any ID?"

Skip was not happy. "No. The Boss never said who it was or why I should let him see the file."

"I see."

Skip downed half his glass of beer and wiped his mouth. "We ain't playing in the minors anymore John."

John nodded. *'You don't know the half of it my friend.'*

***

CHAPTER SIXTEEN

May 7, 2009
IPTF Headquarters
Washington, D.C.

It was five o'clock. Tammy Davidson, Executive Assistant
to the Deputy Director of the IPTF checked her desk
area one last time. A little rush of excitement made her
shiver unexpectedly. In just a few days she would be
Mrs. Tammy Whitehead, wife to the third most powerful
man at the Department of Justice. The United States
Deputy Attorney General, the Honorable Bradley
Shelbourne Whitehead was going to be husband and father
to Tammy and her daughter April.

Not for the first time or the last, Tammy said a silent prayer for her old friend and mentor Dawn Fenstermacher. If not for Dawn's friendship and support, Tammy would still be fetching coffee and making copies in a secure, but dead-end job. When Dawn left their old employer to form Nascent Resources Group Corporation, she had offered Tammy the opportunity to go with her. The risks were huge for Tammy as a single mother. To even think of leaving was crazy. What if the company failed? How would she provide for April? But Dawn had that special light about her. A sense of destiny and purpose emanated from Dawn like a beacon. Despite her fear's Tammy knew she would follow Dawn anywhere. Her heart pounding, Tammy had said yes.

Two years later, Dawn Fenstermacher the creator of the ZIZPRO Protocol and her fledgling company Nascent Resources Group was awarded a multibillion dollar contract from the Federal Government of the United States. Within sixty days, their old employer purchased the firm and Tammy's stock options had made her a wealthy young lady.

Even better, James Dodd, one of the original partners in the company, left to assume the Deputy Directorship for Technology of the Infrastructure Protection Task Force. Dawn, per the terms of the contract, assumed complete responsibility for testing and development of the protocol as Chief of Systems Applications for Nascent Resources Group. A phone call from Dawn to the Deputy Director was all it took for Tammy to land the Executive Assistant position.

Life was funny. One moment you are struggling to get by, then miraculously everything one could dream and hope for is given to you. She wished her friend Dawn could be with her to share her joy.

She fingered the embossed surface of the RSVP from John O'dea. He had added in a little note at the bottom:
Congratulations Tammy!
I will be delighted to attend. John

***

NightWire
May 9, 2009

Matt Frank smiled into the camera.
"We have a special program tonight. We are going to visit the Renaissance. No, we won't be traveling back through time, but we will be visiting the future with a man many are describing as a visionary. Our special guest, Assistant Deputy Director of the IPTF, Jerry Carpenter joins our regular panel as we delve into the mind of the creator of the Renaissance Project.   Good evening Director Carpenter."

Jerry smiled and nodded. "Good evening Matt. Just plain 'Jerry' will do." *'Someday I'll pay that bastard Thurston back for putting me up to this...'*

"Okay Jerry. Most people have at least heard about the Renaissance Project. Renaissance has been by all accounts a smashing success. At last week's press conference, the President said that Renaissance was the 'Crown Jewel' of his administration. Now we have a late breaking story developing from highly placed White House sources that I really want to get to in this segment. A controversial, maybe even explosive announcement by the White House may be imminent. But first, briefly, can you describe for us the work Renaissance has been doing?"

"Yes Matt, I would say that Renaissance is really about helping people to adapt and change. It's about education and restructuring, it's about reaching out to those at risk and in need of guidance and hope. It's about going beyond simply caring, to actually doing positive things, offering hands-on, concrete solutions for real problems. It's about affirmation and victory."

Matt laughed. "Well I think I am beginning to understand the visionary thing, that all sounds rather vague and wonderful at the same time. In this day and age and especially working within a Republican administration you must have your critics. What you have just described seems almost Kennedy-esque if I may say so..."

'Just smile, after all, he is an idiot.' "Not at all Matt, we are quite realistic. In fact, before we entered the new economy, our efforts as a nation to address social problems like: crime, unemployment, drug abuse, and addiction, were unqualified failures. Billions of dollars were being spent annually, spent with literally no measurable success in any initiative. Quite the opposite, we were doing more harm then good."

Matt nodded thoughtfully. "We have certainly seen the fruits of your labors. By all accounts crime has plummeted, our streets are safer and cleaner and many, many people's lives have been changed for the better."

"Thank you Matt. We have been absolutely elated at the progress so far. We know the game is far from over but we have done well in the early innings." *'Come on Matt let's cut to the chase'...*

Jerry watched Matt put on his, I know something you don't know face, that insiders like Jerry always found mildly amusing. *'Who the hell did this clown think he was dealing with? Leaks are almost never leaks. Investigative journalism had been dead for a long time.*

Media "pundits," like poor stupid Matt Frank, performed like trained monkeys. Give them a little tidbit, a little spin so they could understand the issue and off they would run to their cameras or word processors and chatter out a breathless analysis of "what it all meant"--morons.' Jerry kept a straight face as Matt launched his big bombshell.

"Well, standby Jerry, the play book may be changing mid-game. As I alluded to at the beginning of the segment, there has been talk, leaks if you will, that the administration is seriously looking at decriminalizing the use of narcotics. Moreover, there have been proposals floated that would seek to establish retail outlets for the purpose of providing marijuana, cocaine, and even heroin to the general public. Why open that Pandora's box now when we have apparently won the war on narcotics in this country? Are we going to be able to go to the local post office and purchase a roll of stamps and gram of hashish to go? Am I getting this right?"

'You couldn't get it right if I branded it on your forehead.' "First of all Matt, I don't know. I personally have no information on whether or not what you are saying is accurate. I do know that despite our success in cutting off the international trade in illicit narcotics, demand remains high. I do know that there are dangerous even toxic concoctions being smoked, inhaled, ingested and even injected with often-deadly consequences."

"Yeah, but golly molly Jerry,'we're with the government; we're here to help you score'? Do we really want to go there?"

Jerry laughed. *'Trained monkeys could be so damn so cute....'*

"Well let's look at the facts instead of the myths. The prohibition of alcohol in America was a total disaster for the country. Despite prohibition people continued to drink."

"Similarly, during the War on Drugs prior to the new economy, supply was never curtailed despite the massive resources expended to shut off the supply. When we shut off the profit motive, as predicted, we finally shut down the supply and distribution. What we can't eradicate is the demand side of the equation. I don't believe we ever will."

Matt pondered this weightily. "Okay, maybe so, but let me be clear on this. What you seem to be saying is that you, Jerry Carpenter, support not only decriminalization, but you would also support retail distribution of dope by our government?"

Jerry frowned slightly. *'Jesus this is tedious.'*

"Not with great enthusiasm Matt, I personally would prefer that drugs, as well as the desire to use them, could be removed from society, but in the interest of public safety, in the interest of preserving the gains we have made, yes I would. However, I would impose some important caveats. First I would require that the proceeds of the legal sales of these substances be fenced to fund treatment and avoidance education programs."

"Second, I would not allow any formerly controlled substance to be combined with other products, like soft drinks, teas or bakery goods to enhance their appeal or soften the image that what you're doing is using dope."

"Third, there would be no advertising or marketing. I would not permit store displays or attractive packaging.

There would be no licensing or permission to create brand names."

"Fourth, intoxication whether by drug use or alcohol, would continue to have severe consequences in those environments and settings that we have already proscribed for alcohol, driving a car, operating machinery, etc.."

Matt hunched forward hoping he had the proper Larry King grimace. "So in your view, personal responsibility would be required to include severe consequences for inappropriate use in inappropriate situations?"

"Of course." *'No, we should let them run wild in the streets you cretin'.*

Matt looked down at his notes,"going back to your earlier comment about the dangers inherent in a situation where people are potentially harming themselves even more with cockamamie potions and homemade substitutes.
Wasn't prostitution in Nevada legalized decades ago for similar reasons, i.e., public safety with respect to limiting the spread of sexually transmitted diseases etc.?"

'I wonder if he could have thought of this on his own? Probably not'.

"I think that's a useful analogy Matt. Whatever one's personal moral compass dictates, regulating and monitoring legalized prostitution in Las Vegas saves lives. When you add up the financial cost of treatment of sexually transmitted diseases, it also saves money, and keep in mind, the cost of that regulation and monitoring has not been borne by taxpayers. The participants in the activity fund it."

Matt grinned, "well that's a nice way to say it Jerry. Participants in the activity–we used to call them 'Johns'."

Jerry smiled back. "Well...This is a family show isn't it?"

Now Matt put on his 'shrewd appraisal of the situation face'. "It sounds like what you're saying is that perhaps we are evolving or perhaps maturing as a nation? What I mean is, are we learning to deal with human foibles and desires based on a sober and realistic assessment of what is rather than what we might wish for ideally? Are we really ready for this?"

'Idiots like you, you mean?' "That's debatable I'm sure Matt, but yes, overall, I think we are maturing as a society. We are becoming more successful in recognizing what is possible to change given the tools we have been given."

Matt turned to the camera. 'Jerry is a helluva guy. I owe him for this.' "When we return, we will have our panel and your calls. So stick around, I'm Matt Frank and this is NightWire."

***

May 10, 2009
EARL'S I-95 SUPER STOP
Maryland

David Chandler poked listlessly at his "Cup-o-Chili." It had some strange parts in it that...'Don't look you don't want to know' He should have left Boston earlier, stopping for a bite to eat at "Earl's" was more fatigue than hunger.

He had been allowed to take his oral board for his Master's Degree early. "Straight A" students often received a little extra consideration. It had gone well. He was too wound up to wait for morning. He had packed his car and left even though it was already early rush hour in Boston. Now he wondered if that had been such a great idea. *'When your eyes start rolling...'*

"More coffee, Sugar?" David looked up and smiled "Please, thank you."

She poured and smiled at him shyly, "you ain't no trucker are ya honey? Where ya headed?"

David smiled back. "I'm in school, just going home to visit my folks." Her slow sassy southern talk was balm to his soul-not like the harsh nasal tones of Boston.

She straightened up and put one hand her hip. "Oh my, isn't that nice. So where do you call home?"

David looked at her. *'She's obviously as bored as I am tired'.* Except for the cook behind the counter and David, the place was empty. *Okay, I'll play...* "Near Chattanooga, Soddy Daisy actually..."

"Oh, now Ah know where that is," she cried, her voice swooping in triumph.

"You do? Now that is a first. Are you from around there?"

She giggled, "Signal Mountain High School, class of 2004. All-Conference Champions in Football you may recall, three years in a row."

David laughed with her. "Small world ah..."

"Tina"

"Okay Tina, I'm David. How long will it take me to get there from here?"

Tina frowned at her watch. "Well, it all depends on how fast you drive I guess, but I'd get there at least by ten in the mornin'."

David smiled, "how fast do you drive Tina?"

She laughed and pinched his cheek, "like a wild woman," and flounced away, hips swaying, ponytail bouncing.

David laughed and looked at his watch. "Two a.m." he groaned out loud.

'The longer I sit here the longer it will take to get there'. He grunted and stood up, stretching his back and leg muscles. *'She must pull that bit a hundred times a day, still…Lord she was a pretty young girl.'*

Tina pouted at him like a little girl when he got to the register.
"Gotta go huh?"

'If you keep this up, I'll apply for a job here…'
"Yeah Tina, I'm burning moonlight. Can I get a large coffee to go?"

"Sure thing honey." She turned and prepared the coffee.
'What a sucker I am--she doesn't even remember my name…'

Tina handed him the coffee and pulled the guest check from his hand, and with a big wide-eyed grin slowly tore it in two.

"You come back and see me any time David. Drive safe

now, and be sure and tell your folks I said hey."
David was definitely awake now as a tingling tightness
made itself known below.
Face flushed, "Thanks Tina. I'll do that."

He left the restaurant and turned to look at her one more
time as he crossed the parking lot. She waved and actually
blew him a kiss. David laughed and blew one back.
Suddenly he wasn't tired at all.

***

May 11, 2009
The White House
Washington, D.C.

The President had just concluded a brief but emotional
meeting with his National Security Advisor Charles
Etheridge. The topic was the signing and release of two
new Presidential Executive Orders that were sure to rock
the political, legal and cultural foundations of the nation.

Executive Order 363701, Decriminalization of possession
of personal use quantities of narcotics and the
establishment of policies that reflect the proper role of
the Government in dealing with the societal impact of
narcotics use, was, specifically, treatment and education,
vice criminal arrest and incarceration.

The second and related Executive Order 363702
established the guidelines for the provision by the state
of resources, licensing and manufactory for public, over
the counter resale of narcotics, establishing a national
needle exchange program and setting the guidelines for
each. Funding for these initiatives would derive from
revenues collected in the sale of narcotics to the general
public out of government approved and licensed retailing
facilities.
Charles Etheridge had been apoplectic. "Mr. President

you are committing political suicide! I don't know if our little trial balloon got your attention but it sure got mine. This is poison. Do we have to get out front so fast?"

The President had just smiled blandly at his National Security Advisor and replied "Do you think so Charley? Have you ever really thought about what damage we have done to otherwise ordinary people by criminalizing personal behaviors? Are you unaware of the billions upon billions of dollars we have thrown down rabbit holes trying to stop the flow of narcotics into this country?"

"Of course Mr. President, but we won. The pipeline isn't just dry, we severed it!" '*Who cares? Ancient history boss --what's really bothering you?*'

The President got up from his desk and stood looking out over the White House grounds. The Renaissance Centers were backlogged as were the RIDS facilities. The idea was to process people that were not yet enrolled in the new economy. There were at least thirty million of those. The system was strained to the limit. Criminal activity was, other than drug user related crimes, down, way down. If that had not been so, the system would have collapsed under its own weight already. '*I will not risk that.*'

"Yeah Charley we won. Since the new economy there is no question that we have broken the back of the syndicates and cartels. Great. I said we would and we did it. Fine. So what are we seeing now? Pharmacies, clinics, and hospitals are being burglarized and looted from New York to LA. Hell, how about that pharmaceutical warehouse in Grand Rapids, South Dakota for Chrissake - it burned to the ground during a botched burglary attempt?"

The President abruptly turned and scooped a folder off his desk and literally winged it at his National Security

Advisors head, "Look at this shit Charley, Huh? What do you think of this? These are the national intelligence estimates prepared by our own people. Physicians, Nurse Practitioners and Pharmacists are afraid of their patients. They're asking what the hell they're supposed to do to alleviate the demand."

President Waites turned back to the view out his window. "Charley, we are just creating new paradigms for illicit drugs to be procured and distributed and as a result we will continue to put otherwise normal, responsible, tax paying Americans in jail. Well, hooray for us."

Charley watched silently as the President stood motionless at the window.

"But Mr. President, surely there must be some other way."

The President turned around now and fixed Charley with an uncompromising stare.

"No Charley, if we can't stop drug use and abuse with the new economy, what the hell do we do next, start shooting people in the streets?" '*What had Jerry Carpenter said? We're about forty-eight hours ahead of a resource crisis every day. One more push and we'll be in it. You've got to stop clogging the pipes with people that just want to catch a buzz.*'

"Charlie, we have to stop putting people in jail for wanting to smoke a little pot or toot a little cocaine or even, if it's what they need to have, shoot up their heroin. There are people dying out there. They're running around like complete idiots smoking, inhaling, hell, probably drinking half-baked, homemade concoctions that are nothing but mixtures of rat poisons and household solvents, and who the hell knows what else. You read the papers."

The President returned to his desk and slammed each word home with his fist on the blotter,"I'm going to end this insanity and I'm going to END IT NOW!"

Charlie drew back in his chair a little and nervously cleared his throat. '*Okay, I think I get your drift.*'

President Waites cleared his throat and settled back into his chair. '*I hope that little display worked.*'

"The Office of National Drug Control Policy is going to go away."

"Right."

"BATF will execute distribution policy."

"Right."

"Justice will write proposed legislation for when the E.O. expires if I don't renew it for another six months."

"Yes Sir."

"The Governors will be sat down and told to shut the hell up unless they want to be on the wrong side of this and pay for it later. Give that to Bernie."

"Right." '*Bernie you poor bastard.*'

The Chief of Staff will handle Congress.

"Right". '*This should be good. They'll eat the little prick alive. If the Chief of Staff had any balls, he wouldn't have ducked this meeting.*'
RENAISSANCE will take on education and recovery treatment when, and if, they want it.

"Right." '*Why don't we all just go home and let those assholes run the country out in the open? No one else seems to have a say....*'

"That's my decision Charlie. If you can't support it I'll understand."

Charley rose, "you have my full support Mr. President." '*God help us all.*'

***

May 13, 2009
Soddy Daisy, TN

Art said a prayer of thanks as he read again the letter his son had brought to him. It was at John's urging, that David had finally come home from Boston.

Art,
I hope this letter finds you and Betty well. I will be thinking of you all in the days and weeks to come.

How do I begin? I suspect David has thought that somehow I might have held the beliefs of people like you and Betty, to be responsible for what happened to Dawn. I never did.

I have recently learned more than I wanted to know about some of the people I once blindly trusted. I am dealing with that knowledge now.

I've never been much of a religious person. I hope, and if anyone is listening, I pray, that someday we will all get together again. I would like that very much.

John O'dea

Art folded the letter and wiped his eyes. '*David had come home. Nothing else mattered.*'

***

May 14, 2009
United Air Lines
International Flight 933
Somewhere over Missouri

John folded up the tray and settled in for the flight.
Tammy's wedding had been a very private event. Brad
Whitehead was, despite his privileged background, a pretty
down to earth guy. Tammy had cried when she greeted
John at the airport. She had insisted he not take a cab to
the Hotel. *'Oh John, I am so glad to see you. I'm such a
crybaby. I'm sorry.'*

John thought of Dawn as he looked out the window. *'I'm
getting closer Dawn.'*

Tammy had told John things he had not known.
Apparently, last November and December, there had been
several "knock-down, drag-out" fights between Dawn and
the Director of the IPTF, Tim Thurston.

According to Tammy, Dawn had serious misgivings about
the timetable that Thurston was demanding for the
transfer to the new economy. Dawn had argued they
should phase in the system over the next three to five
years.

John had asked why, was there a problem with the
protocol?

"No. Dawn was not afraid the system would fail," Tammy
said. "She had told me she was afraid the technology was
too far out in front of what the government had devised
to protect peoples rights-the potential for abuse
outweighed the benefits. She said she wanted both systems

to coexist side by side for a few years until Congress and the Courts had enough time to set some proper checks and balances."

John had stared at Tammy in amazement. She never said a word about any of this to John.

"Well" Tammy had said, "Tim sure felt awful after what happened."

John had thought '*yeah I bet the bastard was all broken up about it.*'

Then the bombshell, John asked Tammy if she might have ever dealt with a guy named Carl Ennis. Tammy had frowned a little and said "you mean 'C.J.?"

"Yeah." John had said as casually as he could.

"I didn't know you knew C.J. He didn't work with any of us. He wasn't a techy. I thought he had something to do with the Task Force side. I only saw him a couple of times. I think he left sometime before Christmas. Haven't seen him around since then."

"Was he kind of short and fat?"

No. Not at all, C.J. was tall and kind of skinny. "Here look," she rummaged in her purse, "we had a little office party right before Thanksgiving. See, here's me and Brad getting a little schnockered, and here's C.J. by the door. He must have been looking for the Director or something. He never came in. I didn't even know he was there until I got the film developed."

"Can I see?" John took the print from Tammy. '*Stay calm, smile...*' John looked at the face.'*It was him. It had to be.*'

He couldn't believe it. '*This is the bastard that killed Dawn.*'

John cleared his throat. "That's a great picture of you and Brad," he smiled. "Can I keep it?"

"Huh? Oh Thanks. Sure, I always get double prints." She had looked at John curiously. "Not the same guy?"

"No. Like you said, he's tall and thin."

John closed his eyes. The big airliner tracked southwest toward the Gulf of Mexico and the resort Island of Cozumel, Mexico. '*I love you Dawn.*' Despite himself, he slept.

EPILOGUE

In the spring of 2009, a terrible plague was sweeping the nation. The plague was the new economy and it was relentless. But only those who rejected the new economy were affected. Surrender to the new economy was the only path to a cure.

Most Americans stepped over the bodies of the victims with more disgust than pity. It has often been noted that to be marked as different has rarely been a positive distinction in any society. Indeed the victims had made a choice. They could blame no one but themselves for the plight of their condition.

The dwindling remnant of Americans resisting enrollment in the new economy was failing. Some had made preparations equal to the challenges of the change. Most had not.

By marked contrast, for the vast majority of Americans, life was great and getting better. PTA's were in session, husbands and wives became mothers and fathers, promotions, graduations, marriage, divorce, mergers and divestitures, comings and goings, the upward trend of equity and capital markets under the leadership of the new economy continued apace.

For those who had enrolled life was obscenely normal. The obscenity was in contrast to the utter lack of pity they felt for those who had not.

Truly, America in the spring of 2009 was a colossus. Politically, and most of all, economically, there was no rival to American supremacy.

The Eurasian monetary, political and economic crises of the late nineties had revealed the emergent nations of the Pacific Rim, to include the Kleptocracy of the imploding Russian Republic and its former rival China to be shallow pretenders to greatness. The tripartite pact between India, Russia and the People's Republic of China had not altered the reality of their relative weakness economically. The gap would not be closed in this century. Perhaps it never would.

Europe, by contrast, had finally emerged from its twenty-year funk with a new optimism and vibrancy. Like the United States it had dealt with the issues of sweeping technological change by embracing change head-on.

Generally, to the south lay chaos and decay. Africa, South America, and the polyglot of East Asia and Indonesia wallowed in fiscal meltdown amidst political and cultural confusion. The western nations forged ahead on the backbone of complex infrastructure and distribution systems developed over decades of modernization and investment in and adoption of cutting edge technology.

There was talk of the American millennium. Even the European community, at long last, accepted with grace and a growing sense of belonging, a global system shaped and controlled by American economic and political might.

The world acknowledged and paid homage to the 21st century Pax Americana. The President of the most powerful nation on earth was by right, feted as a modern emperor. It was good to be an American again. Like the post year wars following World War Two and again during the late eighties and early nineties of the twentieth century, America was ascendant. The future was exceedingly bright.

For some, those in active resistance to the new economy, the future had withered. Dependence on technology savaged the "POLIREG" movement. Modern Americans were simply not equipped to provide for themselves. Cut off from access to supermarkets and ATMs, modern transportation, and labor-saving appliances and technologies, the resistance movement faced a stark choice. Join the new economy or die in a futile and increasingly unsympathetic cause.

Despite the deck stacked against them, a tiny hard core of resistance remained free. Survivors gathered together in small self-sufficient groups by ones and twos. They prayed for redemption and some it was known and feared, plotted revenge.

American society viewed them all with increasing scorn. The patience of that great and good country America was waning. Political and religious opposition to the new economy was increasingly viewed as dangerously subversive as well as futile. The harvest would soon begin.

***